# *THE POPE*

*Poor Oppressed People Everywhere*

*Author:  Saoul Montalvo*

# ACKNOWLEDGMENT

All praise due to Allah the Most Merciful.

First and foremost, I want to thank my mother because without you, I wouldn't be the man that I am today.

I want to thank my brothers (SHARIF and SHAHID), my sister (SONIA) for reminding me just how important family is.

Shout out to - DAY ONES ROOF, BEICO, SU & FLACCO. Also to DTH and the entire TRIPLETT FAMILY.

Special shout out to ROBERT LABOO aka BAGHDAD JIG and MORE THAN WORDS PUBLICATION.

Lastly but not least, I have to give love to all the brother's who helped me on this journey. There are just too many of you to name but I must say, your advice and encouragement helped me more than you can ever imagine.

I am more than grateful to you all. Allah bless you all.

Much More Than Word Publications


For More Info, Please Contact:

Labooboys@gmail.com

Instagram/forever_jig

*Prologue*

Tonight, would be the last night of Howard Leonard's life. It was a very uneventful life up until a few years ago.

Howard had become famous overnight; well infamous might be a better way to describe him. You see Howard was a police officer and one night while on patrol he came across what he thought was a suspicious looking young man. The fact that the young man was African American had nothing to do with it, well almost nothing. But you could not tell that to the liberal media Howard would later complain.

Oh, and the marchers and protesters did not want to hear anything that old Howard had to say. He was just doing his job he would later say and if the young fella would have just cooperated things might have turned out differently. Howard asked the young man where he was going and could he see some identification, when the kid became "mouthy" as Howard would put it. He started telling Howard to leave him alone and that this was America and that he could walk down the street without being harassed. Well one thing led to another and the next thing Howard knew the kid was dead. In retrospect Howard did not know what happened it was all pretty much a blur. All he knew is that he was on a deserted street with a 6-foot 5-inch black kid.

How in the hell was he supposed to know that the kid was a basketball phenom? A five-star recruit that was on his way to one of the best college teams in the nation.

By the time the media was done with old Howard he was painted as the biggest racist in the world! Just another blood thirsty cop out here killing unarmed black civilians. And that turned out to not be such a bad thing because there were groups that specialized in helping people who found themselves in similar positions. The district attorney was forced to seek an indictment against Howard but with the high price lawyer and P.R firm the group hired Howard walked away looking like the victim.

It goes without saying that the kid's parents and a large portion of the population did not agree with the decision and a few riots broke out.

Howard enjoyed his fifteen minutes of fame and he still got invited to speak at events from time to time.

But he did not make it through completely unscathed because his wife divorced him and his kids' would no longer speak to him. The divorce is what brought him where he was tonight, at his second job, working security at a sporting goods store to pay alimony and child support.

But life was not all bad for old Howard

Because he still had Bunny!

Bunny was a young lady that he had met at a Gentleman's Club. Sure, he had to pay for the time that they spent together but it was well worth it!

Just thinking about her had him aroused.

To the point where he thought about shaking one off right in his car in the parking lot, it wouldn't be the first time he had done it.

Howard started looking through his phone for some of the pictures she had been sending him lately.

He was so caught up with what he was doing that he did not notice the Town & Country minivan next to him door slide open. By now Howard was on the verge of climax when he heard a tap on the window. He had a handful of himself and he scrambled to put his quickly deflating penis back into his pants.

He grabbed his shield and said, "I'm a cop!" It was all he had the chance to say before he realized the man sitting there had what looked like a silenced Mac.11 machine gun. The masked man waved at Howard and to his own surprise he waved back. And at that moment the masked man raised the gun and squeezed the trigger sending round after round into Howards face, neck and chest.

The gunman then got out of the van and stuck a single sheet of paper into the car, it read -

"Justice for Vernon Johnson"

And it was signed by The P.O.P.E

# CHAPTER 1

"*W*hat do we have Connolly?" asked agent Angelica Marrow as she walked through the crowded crime scene.

"Good morning to you too." Connolly said in response before saying. "Deceased white male, multiple gunshot wounds. Also, we found this." he said as he held a Brevard County Sheriff's badge."The victim's name is Howard Leonard."

"The one who shot the basketball player a couple of years ago?" Marrow shot back.

"The same. And we found this." Connolly said as he handed her the note. It was a single typed sheet of paper.

Marrow could not believe that he had struck again. "This asshole is really starting to get on my nerves." she replied walking under the yellow tape.

Connolly walked with her and said,

"Sooner or later he is going to slip up. They all slip up. And when he does we will be there to take him down! He is an attention whore what with all the notes and social media posts ranting and boasting about what he has been able to get away with so far.

Marrow blew out a breath and dropped trying to calm herself. "Speaking of which, look who is trending today."

She held up her cell phone so that he could see the screen. It was a grainy video of the crime scene. Officer Leonard was dead and then his killer turned the camera to himself and spoke.

The masked man said "To some this may look like cold blooded murder, but I consider it justice! An eye for an eye. I am the first of the oppressed to rise up and strike out at my oppressor, but I will not be the last!"

The screen went black and four letters appeared POPE

"Who is this guy because I cannot wait to meet him!" Marrow said, staring at the screen.

## MEANWHILE

Marcus Tanner was currently a couple of thousand feet over the Atlantic Ocean enjoying the breathtaking view.

He had decided to take the scenic route home after his latest successful mission. Marcus was flying solo in the cockpit of his Cessna. On the hour and a half long flight back to his home state of Virginia. He thought a lot about his life over the past few years and what had brought him to this point.

Marcus was a man on a mission, and that mission was to fight for those who could not or would not fight for themselves. He was even ready to give his life for what he believed. Marcus knew that he would leave his mark and that the world would remember his efforts.

Marcus landed his plane at a small airport two miles from his home.

Once he climbed out of the plane and secured his gear, he got on his dirt bike and made his way home. He gunned the bike down a lonely stretch of highway and turned onto a path that was all but hidden from the road. He followed the path for about a half a mile through the thick woods and came to a stop.

Here in a clearing in the middle of the woods Marcus got off his bike. There was a tarp camouflaged with bushes, so that if you did not know it was there you would walk right pass it. And that was the point. He covered his bike and walked several feet before he took out his cell phone. He quickly typed in a code. Whirring noise and a hum could be heard as the ground rose revealing an entrance with a pair of stairs heading down to his "home".

Marcus descended the stairs and hit a button which closed the door behind him.

The bunker that Marcus called home was built by his father. Marcus being an engineer in college and a member of the Army Corps of Engineers, he made some additions to his father's original design. Marcus turned on his computer and quickly found what he was looking for, news about himself.

*"Today federal and local authorities across the country have joined forces in the biggest manhunt in U.S history.*

The subject of the manhunt is the man known as the POPE. Not the beloved Pontiff who resides in Vatican City, but a ruthless killer who has killed five police officers to date and he is suspected in the murder of another.

The killing spree which has terrorized the country for members of law enforcement involved in police shootings of unarmed citizens.

The latest victim was Howard Leonard, a Brevard County Sheriff officer, who was gunned down outside of the sporting goods store where he was working a second job.

Howard was accused of killing an unarmed teen named Vernon Johnson, a young basketball star with a promising future. A grand jury failed to indict Howard, sparking several days of unrest in Florida after the announcement.

All the victims have in common are that they were either found not guilty by a jury or the grand jury failed to indict in the shooting of an unarmed civilian.

The **POPE** is an acronym for,

**Poor**

**Oppressed**

**People**

**Everywhere.**

He sees himself as an avenging angel, but law enforcement sees him as nothing but a cold-blooded murderer."

The shot of the reporter is replaced by one of an older man in a dark suit. He is the Director of the FBI.

"Today every agent under my command has a directive that nothing or no one else is more important than the capture or killing of this individual. It is a slap in the face of our great nation and to all those men and women across the country that put on the uniform daily to protect us all. So, the fact that he has decided to target these brave men and women is a personal affront and I plan to deal with it as such. Thank you."

Marcus turned the sound down as the man walked away from the podium.

As Marcus sat there, he became lost in his thoughts.

## MANY YEARS EARLIER

It was a beautiful May afternoon and ten-year-old Marcus was playing in the backyard with his little brother Michael.

"Mikey you have to poke holes in the top like this, so that he can get some air."

Marcus told his baby brother about the butterfly that they had trapped in the mason jar.

Marcus got a nail and poked holes in the lid of the jar. He took his job as a big brother very seriously and he looked out for Mikey and taught him everything that his ten year old mind knew.

"Come here Mikey let me tie your shoe and make sure you don't get dirty 'cause if you do momma will skin us both!"

The boy's father stood on the back porch of the family home and watched his boys. Michael senior loved them more than he thought humanly possible.

His wife of fifteen years Andrea walked out and kissed him on the cheek and called to her two sons. "Get in this house and get cleaned up before we go to your grandparent's house."

The two boys hustled in the house without being told another word.

A short time later the family all got into the car for the short drive to visit their grandparents. Marcus loved going because his grandfather would always tell him stories about what it was like being in what he called the "Great War". He would show Marcus his gun collection, but he would never allow him to touch them.

Marcus was so busy thinking about the fun he was going to have today that he did not hear his mother talking to him from the front seat.

"Marcus Elliot Tanner I know you hear me talking to you!"

"Yes, momma?" was his quick reply.

"When you get to your grandparents house you better not start bugging your grandfather about his old dusty gun collection." It was as if she could read his mind. His dad was behind the wheel. He saw his father's eyes in the mirror and his dad winked, and

12

Marcus knew that he would get a chance to look at all his grandfather's cool stuff. Marcus looked at his little brother who had dozed off and was drooling on his nice clean shirt. Marcus wiped his baby brother's chin off and smiled at him. When they reached their destination, Marcus was out of the car in a flash with Mikey trailing to keep up.

"How are my little soldiers doing today?" asked Marcus's Grandfather David.

"We're good grandpa." they both said smiling.

"Well that's good, now get on in the house and let your grandmother get a look at you."

They spent the entire day with their grandparents, and they loved every bit of it. After dinner Marcus and his grandfather headed for the garage where he kept all of his cool stuff from the war.

"Marcus my boy I know that you are only 15 years-old but I think you would make a mighty fine soldier!"

Marcus knew his grandfather was only teasing him.

"Grandpa I'm only 10"

"You sure? Because you are mighty big for a 10-year-old? Well anyway when I was in the war, I was only 18 years old. Now that may seem like a lot to you right now but before you know it you will be 18 too. Now don't get me wrong and think that I am saying war is right. Because it is not but sometimes it is necessary.

Sometimes you have no choice but to fight. And when you become committed to it there is nothing that can stop you!"

Marcus hung onto his grandfather's every word. "You see this right here?" he said holding up a rifle with a bayonet." I took this from the first man that I killed in the war" he said looking seriously at the boy.

"We were eye to eye. If I did not kill him, he was going to kill me and the rest of my platoon." Marcus' eyes were wide with fascination as he listened to his grandfather's story.

"So, what happened?"

"We fought for our lives. I took this bayonet and I killed him with It." he said simply."There is not a day that goes by when I don't think about that night and what happened. I still see that young man's face. But I knew that what we were doing was right! It was necessary, so I do not regret the choice that I made because there was no choice."

"My daddy was in the war too right?"

His grandfather paused and thought for a second before replying.

"Yes, he was in a different war. He was a sniper. I still have his rifle around here somewhere. Some people, including your father did not think that the war they fought was necessary. They sent a lot of young men over there to die and he still does not know why so it affected him differently than the war did me. Can you understand that?" Marcus nodded. "One of these days you may

14

be faced with the possibility of fighting in a war, just make sure that it is a cause that you truly believe in."


### LATER THAT EVENING

On the drive home Marcus was still thinking about all of the things his grandfather told him.

"Marcus you are very quiet, is everything alright." his mother asked

"Yes, ma'am. I am just a little bit tired that's all." Marcus knew that his mother would be upset and would not want him to look at his grandfather's stuff anymore, so he kept the conversation to himself. Mikey was curled up in the backseat with his thumb in his mouth, like he always did when he was asleep.

Marcus was starting to drift off as well when he was startled awake by the sounds of screeching tires. The car they were in was broadsided and they flipped over. The force of the impact was enough to send them flipping over and over. Marcus was bouncing around in a blizzard of glass and metal but he was held in place by his safety belt.

It seemed like they were flipping forever and when they finally came to a stop the car was on its side. It was deathly quiet for a few seconds. The sound of his father's voice broke the silence.

"Marcus! Marcus can you hear me?" Was the first thing he heard when he regained consciousness.

"Marcus, are you alright?" his father asked as he reached for his son.

As Marcus's vision became clearer, he could see that his father was bleeding very badly. He had managed to get out of the mangled wreck. Marcus was still a little bit groggy and it took him awhile to realize what had happened.

He looked around the car and he saw his mother still in her seat strapped in with her seat belt, her neck bent at an unnatural angle and he knew something was wrong right away.

"Mommy!" he began to scream in a panicked state. He tried to help her. "Mommy, Mommy get up!" He pleaded.

His father worked to pull him from the wreckage, and he fought against him. It was then that he looked to the seat next to him and saw that it was empty. A chilling thought entered his mind.``Where's Mikey?" He looked again at the spot his brother occupied only a short time ago as if that might make him reappear. "Dad let me go I have to find Mikey! I have to get Mikey!" he screamed at the top of his lungs as his father was finally able to free him from the car. Marcus was kicking and screaming "Let me go I have to find Mikey!" He was able to fight his father off and he ran around frantically trying to find his little brother. He ran down the middle of the debris filled road and saw something that his terror filled mind would never forget. It was Mikey! He ran as fast as his ten-year-old legs could carry him. His heart felt like it would burst with every step as he got close enough to see just how bad his little brother was hurt.

He ran to his brother and wrapped him in his arms and said "Oh Mikey! It will be alright Mikey!" He hugged his brother as if squeezing him as tight as he could, would bring him back to life. But Mikey was gone and Marcus knew it. But that did not stop him from trying to get some life back into his battered, broken little body. Marcus sat in the middle of the road hugging Mikey oblivious to everything around him. As the sirens wailed in the distance Marcus and his father were both in shock.

The first officer on the scene ran to the car that had hit Marcus and his family and said, "Oh My God Billy!" He quickly jumped on his radio "We have an officer down! I repeated the officer down!"

He gave them his location as other cars began to arrive. The mood became tense. Michael had pulled his deceased wife from the car and was holding on to her, when one of the officers charged him."You dirty son of a bitch!" He said and rushed Michael and kicked him in the face. The mob of angry cops rushed Michael and began to viciously attack him. The whole time they were beating him he was looking into his dead wife's eyes.

Marcus saw what was happening to his father and knew he had to help.

"Mikey, I got to go help Daddy." That was the only way he could leave his brother's side. He ran full speed and charged into the crowd. **"DADDY!"**

He screamed and dove on top of his father in an attempt to help ward off some of the blows that were raining down on his father. The sight of the little boy was not enough to stop the blood thirsty cops from the revenge they sought.

It was only when the paramedics arrived and intervened did the police stop the assault. If they did not interrupt the police, it was a very real chance that Michael may have been beaten to death.

While the paramedics tended to the injured officer, Michael was handcuffed and bleeding on the side of the road.

Marcus was in the back seat of a police car looking at his family or what was left of his family.


### HOURS LATER

*This can't be happening.* Marcus thought to himself as he waited in the crowded emergency room. The only parent Marcus had left was handcuffed to a gurney while being guarded by an army of angry police officers. Michael was in very bad shape. He was bleeding from numerous wounds from his face and head and one of his eyes was swollen completely shut. "I hope you die nigger!" One officer hissed.

Although Marcus could not hear what the officer said from where he sat, he could read his lips. This made him even more afraid, he could not lose his father too. Michael hadn't received medical treatment because all of the medical staff was focused on saving the cop who had killed his family.

"We have to get him to surgery STAT!" The attending physician yelled and with that officer William Reeves was wheeled away.

Only once their fellow comrade was stabilized did the cops allow doctors to help Michael. Who was busy watching the stretcher carrying his wife and son's killer being wheeled away. Michael was praying with all of his heart and soul that officer William Reeves died on the operating table.

Marcus watched as doctors and nurses converged around his father. But several police officers remained with their prisoner while the majority followed officer Reeves up to surgery to continue their vigil.

"Don't ya'll work too hard ya' hear?" one the officers remarked as he stared at Michael.

It was all too much for Marcus to bear as his young mind began to shut down. He thought about the life he had only a few short hours ago when he and Mikey were outside catching butterflies. He wished that he could stay there and live in that moment forever. It seemed like a lifetime ago. The misery and despair that had become his life were kept at bay by these precious memories. Marcus was snapped out of his thoughts by a very familiar and welcoming voice.

"I am Ruth Tanner and I am looking for my son and his family." Marcus heard his grandmother say.

"Well there ain't much of a family left." one the officers replied.

The remark was enough to send his grandfather into a frenzy because Marcus had never heard his grandfather so upset before. "I will not stand here and listen to your ignorant redneck mouth any longer! Either you tell me where my son and his family are or I will tear this hospital apart until I find them!"

Through all of the commotion cooler heads prevailed when the attending physician returned and replied,

"Excuse me Mr. and Mrs. Tanner, will you follow me please?" The doctor led the distraught parents to their son who was being attended to at the present moment. Not to mention being guarded by the police.

Seeing her son in such bad shape was enough to break his mother down and she began to weep loudly. "I am afraid that your son and his family were involved in a horrific car accident and your son and your grandson were the only survivors."It was almost too much for them to bear. Michael's father had to hold up his wife because it seemed as if she was on the brink of collapse. It took a second for what the doctor said to finally set in.

"Doctor, you said our grandson survived? Well, which one and where is he?"

"He is right over there." the doctor replied as he led the way to where Marcus was sitting.

When he saw his grandparents he raced to them and jumped in their arms.

"It's okay baby." his grandmother said into his ear as she held him tightly but they both knew that everything was not "okay" and it never would be again.


*PRESENT DAY FBI HEADQUARTERS*

*QUANTICO VIRGINIA*

"Listen up ladies and gents we have a very special guest with us today to help us catch the man we know as the POPE. This man needs no introduction, but I will give him one anyway. Mr. Stanley Roberts of Behavioral Science."

With that the Special Agent in Charge moved aside as an average sized, balding man stepped to the podium.

"I am honored that I was asked here to help with this very important investigation." Mr. Roberts replied to the 43 agents in attendance."I will not bore you by giving you my credentials and qualifications, but it is my job to create psychological profiles of people such as the one that you are hunting now. It is my opinion that the unknown subject or UN-SUB is a very intelligent individual. I believe that he is educated and most likely graduated at the very top of his class. I say that because he is an over achiever and it would not be enough for someone like him to just earn a degree. He would have to be the best. And yes, he is male. More specifically a black male! He is between 25 and 30 years of age. I would also say it is a pretty safe bet to say that he is law enforcement."

This comment caused a stir in the audience; they were dead silent hanging on his every word until then.

"Or at the very least he has educated himself in the way that we operate. But if I had to bet on it I would say that he was a cop somewhere in the not too distant past because of the age I placed him at. There is something about the way that he moves and his choice of weaponry that suggest at least to me that our un-sub is also ex-military. Think about the San Diego incident. Our guy took on four armed veteran police by himself and walked away without a scratch. And we all know what happened to the four officers don't we?"

Mr. Roberts was referring to an earlier incident where four officers were slain in a gun battle with the POPE.

"I also believe that our un-sub is a loner. But I also think that he is highly functional in a social setting. Meaning, I don't think that he is a recluse hiding out in Wyoming, but, that he is right now at this moment buying a Frappuccino from Starbucks. Or he is buying underwear from Wal-Mart. This guy blends into a crowd. He is the guy that his neighbor least expects to be our guy. One last thing before I wrap this up people. I think that this is one of the most dangerous men to ever step foot in this country because he is a fanatic who thinks that he is Right! He thinks that he has justice on his side. And I think we all knew that he is not going down without a fight...."

Roberts paused for effect and looked around the room and made eye contact with every agent present before he continued.

"But he is wrong about justice being on his side. We are the Justice and we are going to squash this fucker like a bug!"

### MEANWHILE

Marcus was not at Starbucks or Wal-Mart for that matter, he was outside the residence of one Gregory Mitchoski.

Marcus hit a button on his phone and seconds later the owner of the house was on the line.

"I'm outside." was all Marcus said before clicking off the line. Moments later the front door of the non-descript house opened and a hulking mountain of a man emerged. As Marcus walked up the stairs Gregory's smile spread across his face.

"This is a pleasant surprise." Gregory stated in a heavy Russian accent as he palmed Marcus' hand in his own massive paw.

"The pleasure is all mine Marcus." stated returning Gregory's bright smile.

The two men entered the house and wasted no time getting down to business.

"What can I do for you today?"

"I was in the area and I thought I would stop by just to see what was on today's menu." Marcus shot back.

"Well you are in luck comrade because I have something that not too many people in your fine country have yet."

Gregory typed a few commands into his computer and an image appeared on the screen of a man holding some type of assault weapon.

"What you are looking at is the world finest weapon. It is called an AA12 shotgun. It is the deadliest gun ever made. But if you don't believe me, watch for yourself."

And with that Gregory hit a button and the demonstration began with the man holding the gun in one hand and the clip in another. He held the clip at an angle where it was possible to see the rounds that were loaded into the clip. The rounds resembled shotgun shells but they were longer and skinnier. The man slammed the clip home and pointed the gun at the targets that had been set up for the demonstration. He squeezed the trigger and the gun roared to life and all but shredded the targets. The man then dropped the spent clip from the gun in exchange for a drum that contained 100 rounds. Marcus could see that the shells inside the drum were a different color and he said,

"What's with the different color shells?"

"I am glad you asked that comrade. Those are exploding shells! Very nasty indeed."

The show continued as the man aimed and fired at a wooden door and it exploded on contact. The video cut to a scene in which the shells were shown in super slow motion as they were fired and to

Marcus's amazement he could see as the shells were fired a little propeller came out the back of the shell and it flew at the target and exploded.

"Alright I'm sold!" Marcus said having seen enough.

"I also have new lightweight body armor. Very tough, very strong, and you can run very fast and have great mobility." The big Russian said getting excited.

"OK I will take several of both. Also, I will be needing the items I requested the last time we spoke"

"I already have them ready to ship. Will everything still be going to the same place?"

"Yes, and I want them sent ASAP." Marcus said thinking to himself that he could not wait to play with his new toys.

"Tanner Industries how may I help you?" Replied Marcus secretary, Tanya. "Hold on Mr. English he has been waiting for your call. Mr. Tanner line one." Tanya said into the intercom.

Marcus spoke to the man for a few minutes and then ended the call. Right now, he was in the middle of putting together his next mission.

He knew that he was the federal government's number one target right now. And they knew his pattern by now. It was a possibility that they could be waiting for him when he went to the next target, but the sad thing was that there were so many police shootings spread out across the country that they had too much ground to cover. Marcus was brought out of his thoughts by Tanya knocking on his door.

"Yes Tanya, come in."

"I signed for those deliveries that you have been waiting for Mr. Tanner."

"Thank you, Tanya. Will you do me a favor? Hold my calls, and I will be working through lunch so order me my usual from Kelsey's."

"Alright Mr. Tanner."Tanya said then exited the same way that she had come.

Marcus went to his workstation and saw the packages stacked on the floor. Marcus owned Tanner industries; part of what he did there was to be a defense contractor to the United States government. A few years back Marcus created something that had saved many lives including his own. It was called an Explosion Muffling Device or EMD.

It was a device that was placed over the bomb and it would block the radio signal of the bomber. And if by chance it did go off it would reduce the killing power by 50%. That fact alone saved many lives in war zones like Iraq where they had to deal with roadside bombs. Marcus was an expert in the field and his invention had made him a rich man. So, now the government paid him to come up with the next big thing, But Marcus had different ideas in mind nowadays.

"All rise. The Honorable Judge Pitts presiding."

With that the jam packed court room was filled to capacity with police and police sympathizers. Today was the first court appearance for Michael who was charged with two counts of vehicular homicide and aggravated assault on a police officer. When it came time for Michael to make his appearance his family and friends were shocked beyond belief of what they saw. Michael was nothing but skin and bones! His cheeks were sunk to the point that he resembled a holocaust survivor. His skin was a sickly, ashy color of gray. His mother, Ruth, was thankful that she did not bring Marcus to court with her that day. Michael was shackled and surrounded by a contingent of law enforcement officers. Michael's parents hired their son, a lawyer who was now standing by his side. After the state and Michael's lawyer both stated their names for the record the proceedings got under way.

"Mr. Tanner is a menace who not only threatened his family's life and ultimately cost his young son and his wife their lives. But he gravely wounded a police officer in the commission of his duties. This man is a danger to society and to himself and it is my belief that his bail should represent just how dangerous this animal is!"

"I object to your honor. Those remarks are uncalled for and highly offensive to my client and his family. "Michael's judge was quick to say, "Sustained. Carry on Mr. Oswald but be careful of the words that you use in my courtroom." The judge admonished the prosecutor.

"I think that it is entirely reasonable to set bail at two million dollars."

The courtroom was a mixture of cheers and moans when bail was requested.

Some did not think that the excessively high bail was enough, and they let their displeasure be known.

"Mr. Caldwell, is there anything you would like to say on your client's behalf?"

"Yes, and thank you for your Honor. My client is an upstanding member of the community and a veteran with two tours of duty in Vietnam. The fact he is here being charged with an absurd crime is a gross negligence on the part of the Virginia state police in an attempt to seek revenge for a tragic accident or it could be a cover up!"

"Objection!" Mr. Oswald jumped to his feet so fast you would have thought he was scolded by hot water.

"Mr. Caldwell sticks to the facts." the judge warned.

"Yes, your Honor. The facts of the case are this, my client was t-boned by a police cruiser traveling at a high rate of speed and my client lost his wife and his youngest son. My client now is a single parent with a ten-year-old who is also a survivor of that horrific accident. The trauma that young man has already endured is unimaginable; I don't think that he should suffer any longer without the only parent that he has left in the world."

The judge was quiet for a while as he reflected on what he just heard in his courtroom. "I agree with the need to protect the public from dangerous individuals, but I am also sympathetic to the needs of a little boy who needs his father and some sort of stability in a traumatic situation such as this. So with that said I will set bail at $500,000." That was all that needed to be said and the courtroom turned into a zoo! The police that were present were not happy by such a low bail. " This piece of shit kills his wife and kid and almost kills one of us and he gets out on 500k?" One of the red-faced cops yelled incredulously.

"Order in the court! Bailiff brings in the next case."

Michael's parents were ecstatic! They knew that they would be able to raise the bail money and that Michael would be out soon. As Michael was being led out of the courtroom, he made eye contact with his parents and they made a reassuring gesture and Michael simply nodded.

Later that evening Michael was released from the county jail. His parents were there to pick him up in the parking lot. He was released along with several other inmates so his family did not see him right away. Once they spotted him in the crowd they made their way to him as fast as they could and wrapped him in a loving embrace.

"My baby I am so glad that you are finally out of that awful place!" Ruth said as she hugged her only son.

David looked at his son for the first time and he did not like what he saw.

"Listen to me boy, you have been through the worst thing that a man can go through, but you are going to have to find the strength to pull yourself together! Your boy is counting on you!"

The mention of his son was enough to snap him out of the trancelike state he was in. When he finally spoke for the first time all he said was, "I'm alright just take me to my son." He quietly got into the backseat of his father's Oldsmobile.

The ride home was awkward to say the least. Once they arrived there Michael walked into the house silently.

When his parents were alone David said, "I don't like the look in that boy's eye one bit!"

"David doesn't ridicule what he has been through a lot these last few days. All he needs is some rest and some of my home cooking." Ruth thought that her cooking could fix anything, but she was not naïve, she did not like the way her son looked either.

"Ruth, I mean it. The last time I saw men with that look in their eye was during the war." David replied looking toward the house. Marcus was standing next to his father who was holding a bag containing some of Marcus's clothes.

The next-door neighbor was babysitting, and she wore a worried expression on her face."It's alright, Vera. And thank you." she said to the young woman before she walked away.

"Where are you taking that boy at this time of the night Michael?" Ruth said as calmly as she could.

"We are going home." Michael simply stated.

"Baby I don't think that is such a good idea. I was hoping that you two could stay here awhile and let me nurse you back to health."

"Ma, I'm alright. The only thing I want to do is to take my son home."

"But babe-" was all Ruth could say before David cut her off.

"Ruth the man has a right to take his son home. You spoke your piece and he still wants to go home so we will go along with his wishes. Just know that we are here for you if you need us for anything." David started looking his son in the eye.

Marcus was quiet while everyone spoke oblivious to how what was being said would affect the outcome of his life for years to come.

David chose to drive them home while his wife went in the house and rested, and he wanted a chance to speak to his son in private. When they pulled in front of the house David looked at his son and then his grandson who was in the backseat." Son I won't insult your intelligence and say I know how you feel right now. Because no man should feel what you are feeling right now. But whatever you are feeling or thinking you can always come to me. I will always be here for you."

Michael acknowledged his father's words by turning to face him in the front seat. He slowly nodded his head and grabbing his father's hand in his own and,

"I know dad. I just need some time." And with those words he got out of the car and reached into the backseat, picked up his son and carried him into the dark house.

Michael carried Marcus into the house and sat down on the couch with his son curled up in his lap. The smells of the house were almost too much for Michael to bear. His senses were overcome with the smells of his family. He could still smell his wife's perfume. He could smell the last meal that she cooked for her family. For the first time since this whole ordeal Michael began to cry.

He cried and hugged Marcus as if both of their lives depended on it. As his sobs racked his body his anguished screams were enough to awaken little Marcus. Michael looked into his son's eyes and said "I love you. Please, no matter what happens from this day forward don't ever forget that I love you." Marcus would never forget this moment it would remain carved into his mind for the rest of his days. But he would not be able to convince himself that his father loved him for a very long time…

"Marcus on your feet!" He heard this and it was almost enough to make him piss his pants. Marcus jumped up to see his father standing over him dressed in sweatpants and a t-shirt.

"I am going to give you exactly 10 minutes to get yourself together and meet me in the backyard!" Marcus was in a daze and did not know exactly how to respond. "Now mister move it!" Michael shouted and Marcus scrambled upstairs to get ready.

When he made it in the yard exactly eight minutes later Michael was there. "From this day forward, you are a man." Michael stated like it was the most normal thing in the world to say to your ten-year-old son. "So, I will teach you how to be a man and most importantly I will treat you like a man." Marcus was scared out of his mind because he had never seen his father like this before." With everything that is going on it is not promised that I will be around to raise you myself. But it is my job to teach you to be a man, but not only a man but A BLACK MAN! Living in the most racist country on the planet! I will teach you everything that you need to know. I will provide you with everything you will need until you learn to provide for yourself. But I will never ever take it easy on you…because America won't take it easy on you! Let's begin!"

# CHAPTER 2

## PRESENT DAY CHICAGO, ILLINOIS

"Get your little asses off my corner." The man sneered from behind the wheel of his police cruiser. The young men gathered on the corner listening to rap music were all suddenly filled with fear because they knew exactly who they were looking at. Officer Jake Pugsley.

Officer Pugsley liked what he saw in the group of young men. Fear!" If I come back through here and I see any of you little fuckers tonight you won't have to worry about going to jail because you will be going to the hospital and that's if you are lucky! Now get the fuck out of here!" The crowd quickly dispersed.

"See partner that's how you got to handle these little animals." Jake replied talking to his young partner of the last few weeks." See Maloney, fuck all that bullshit they teach you in the academy that shit will get you killed in Chi-Town. Oh I forgot *Chi-Raq!* See even the lil monkeys know it's a fuckin' war zone out here now. But they know better than to fuck with me, you can bet that!" Jake said with a menacing look on his face. Officer Maloney was in awe of Pugsley. Jake Pugsley was a legend in the Chicago Police Department and that was way before the "incident".

Officer Pugsley was involved in a police shooting of an unarmed suspect that some deemed an execution. The incident involved a man named Taquan Harris who was an ex-con who was wanted on an outstanding parole violation. The two men crossed paths at a notorious Southside watering hole known as the Village Inn. Mr. Harris got into a scuffle inside the bar and was escorted outside by the bouncers who he then began to fight. It was that moment the police were called and as fate would have it Jake Pugsley was the first on the scene. Jake seeing the fight in full swing could not wait to get in on the action and he swung his baton clearing a path until he got to the main event, which was Mr. Harris. By this time Harris was already beaten senseless by three bouncers. The bouncers saw Jake swinging his club and got out of the way, but Mr. Harris did not have that benefit because both of his eyes were swollen shut. So, when he felt Jake grab him from behind, he swung a wild roundhouse right that landed squarely on his jaw, knocking him on the ground. By this time a crowd of onlookers took in the drunken brawl and most of them had their phones out to record the melee. Jake shook off the blow and got back to his feet as the crowd pointed and laughed at him. This was enough to push him to the boiling point. Mr. Harris was being held by several other officers at this point who had arrived on the scene only moments earlier. Jake grabbed Harris by the throat and forced him to the ground. Harris fell to the ground but not before taking Jake down with him.

Jake landed on top and quickly pinned him down using his knees.

Harris knowing the fight was over had one more act of defiance left in him.

Beaten, bloody and battered, Harris shook a bloody wad of phlegm and spit in officer Pugsley's face! In a blind rage Jake Pugsley pulled his weapon and placed it against Harris's head and pulled the trigger, and the cameras caught it all! People were outraged all-across the country as the image of a white police officer killing an unarmed black man exploded across social media.

Jake was placed on modified duty while

An internal affairs unit "looked into" the matter. And after that investigation it was ruled that what Jake did was justified given the circumstances in which the incident took place.

And just like that Jake Pugsley was back on the street and the legend of Jake Pugsley grew like wildfire!

Cops wanted to be like him, and criminals were afraid of him.

It was the end of the shift and Jake and Officer Maloney pulled into the station house and parked their police cruiser.

"This is what it is all about rookie, making it back to punch out for the day!"Jake stated as he made his way back to the trunk to grab the rest of his gear."Any day where you make it home in one piece is a good day! Ain't that right Danny boy?"Jake asked Maloney but got no response. Jake slammed the trunk of the car shut and turned around and did not like what he saw one bit. A man dressed in black and wearing a black mask was holding Maloney at gunpoint. The masked man stood behind Maloney with a silenced pistol to his head."You have got to be kidding me, right? This is some kind of sick joke? What are you trying to rob two cops in the parking lot of a police station? You fuckin' niggers get dumber and dumber every day I swear!'" The masked man only said a few words as he now pointed the gun at Jake. "Justice for Taquan Harris!" Jakes blood froze in his veins as he heard the gunman utter those words because he knew what that meant. Jake saw the muzzle flash and the last thing he thought was "This must be that guy the news has been blabbing about." And with that thought his brain was blown all over the back of his car.

### SEVERAL HOURS LATER

The crime scene was one of the most hectic Agent Marrow had seen in years.

"Tell me something good." she said to the Agent as soon as she was under the tape.

"I will tell you something more than good I will make your fucking day! We have a living witness that saw the whole thing."

Agent Marrow was jet lagged from her flight from out of Washington to Chicago so this was news to her ears.

"I knew that smug bastard would make a mistake sooner or later. Now it's time to make him pay! This scene becomes all too familiar, a dead cop, shot down like a dog in the street. And this one was shot down in the parking lot of a police station for god sakes!" Marrow said venting as she processed the grizzly scene.

Jake Pugsley was in a seated position with his back against the bumper of the squad car. There was a large hole in the center of his forehead and Agent Marrow guessed an even bigger one in the back where the bullet exited. It was something different about this scene.

"He didn't leave his calling card." Marrow said

"Yeah, I know. What are you thinking?" Connolly asked his partner.

"I think we need to go and have a talk with our witness."

They drove to the hospital as quick as they could in the heavy traffic. When they arrived at the Cook County medical center they were escorted to Maloney's room.

"What happened to him? Why is he in the hospital?" Marrow asked the attending physician. "He was unconscious and unresponsive; thanks to a heavy sedative he was given."

"Sedative?" the doctor nodded.

"He was given a heavy dose of propofol."

Connolly shot his partner a look.

"Yes, it is a powerful anesthetic commonly used in operating rooms in most hospitals, but most people know it as the drug that Michael Jackson overdosed with."

"Did he say anything when he was brought in?" Marrow asked

"As I said before he was still heavily sedated."

"May we speak with him now?" Agent Marrow asked.

"Right this way."

When the agents entered the room Maloney was having his blood pressure checked by a nurse.

"Officer Maloney, I am Agent Marrow and this is Agent Connolly of the FBI and we would like to ask you a few questions about what happened last night?" Officer Maloney simply nodded his head and tried to avoid making eye contact.

"What do you remember?"

"It was the end of our shift and Jake was telling me as he always did that punching out at the end of the day is the most important part of the job."Maloney stared off into outer space as he relived the events of a few hours ago."Jake was in the trunk grabbing his gear when all of a sudden someone crept up on me and put a hand over my mouth and a gun to my head."

"At any point did you get a chance to see what the perp looked like?" Connolly said and instantly regretted it.

Maloney's face reddened and tightened up into a mask of anger. "I already told you the asshole grabbed me from behind and before you ask me NO there was nothing I could have done differently."

Marrow saw that he was on the defensive and she said, "No one is saying you did anything wrong. We just really need your help so that we can catch the guy who did this."

This seemed to work because Maloney once again started telling what happened.

"Like I was saying he had a hand over my mouth and that's when Jake turned and saw what was happening. Jake thought it was some kind of joke or something. It was almost like he could not believe that someone would try a stunt like that in the middle of a police station parking lot."

"Did the gunman and Jake say anything to one another?"

"Jake said something about niggers being dumb for trying to rob a couple of cops in a police station or some crap like that."

Marrow could see that he was a little embarrassed by this, so she said,

"It's okay. My dad was a beat cop in Detroit, so I know all about how the old school cops talk to one another."

This made him feel better and he continued.

"The guy with the gun seemed unfazed by what Jake said to him. He only said a couple of words before he shot Jake."

Agent Marrow was on the edge of her seat waiting on the answer to the question she was about to ask but deep down she already knew.

"What did he say, exactly?"

Maloney made eye contact for the first time since their arrival and he said,

"Justice for Taquan Harris."

After leaving the hospital the agents realized they were still stuck at square one. Officer Maloney couldn't tell them anything they didn't already know because as soon as he shot Pugsley he stuck a syringe into Maloney's neck. He was found a short time later right by his now deceased partner. Agent Marrow was behind the wheel of their car when she saw something that made her jam on the brakes.

"What the fuck Marrow!" Connolly screamed as he spilled the hot coffee he was drinking. Marrow ignored him and ran across the street to a vendor who was selling t-shirts. It was what was on the shirts that had her full undivided attention. It was a picture of a bullet riddled cop car with a caption that read *POPE 7 COPS 0.*


## SEVERAL YEARS EARLIER

It was the crack of dawn and Marcus was up and out of bed already. This had become his daily routine for the last seven years. It had been seven years since he lost both of his parents.

His mom was dead and at least that was something he could cope with but the situation with his father was worse.

Marcus had to watch as the man he used to love and look up to become a shell of himself. It was ruled that the accident that killed his mother and brother was a tragic accident and the charges were dismissed but the damage was already done. Michael was a changed man and those changes affected his son the most. He forced Marcus to wake up every morning and do his chores which included cleaning the entire house, going to the store his dad owned and stocking the shelves and opening the store in the morning. All before he went to school. Marcus was not allowed to watch TV or listen to the radio.

Michael gave Marcus books to read and he expected him to write lengthy essays about them. By the time Marcus was twelve he knew all about Malcolm X, MLK and the Black Panther Party as well as the man he was named after, Marcus Garvey.

Michael believed that television and all forms of pop culture would indoctrinate his son with the evil of the "white man's world " as he was fond of saying.

One time, Marcus asked his father why he could not watch TV anymore and he told him.

"So the only things you will see are the things you could never be if you watched TV all day. They dangle these images in your face every day and you become addicted to them, so you watch more and more. Soon that is all you want to do, and you become lazy. Then you feel like the world should be as it is depicted on TV, but it never is. Especially for Black Men in this country."

The only time Marcus was allowed to interact with kids his age was when he went to school. But because he was limited in his interaction with other kids he was socially awkward.

But as Marcus entered his senior year of high school he began to look forward to going away to college. This was a big change for him because up until this point the prospect of being in a strange environment frightened him to no end. The main reason Marcus wanted to go away to school, although he did not want to admit it, was to get away from his dad. His father isolated himself from the rest of the world and the only one he had to take his frustration out on was Marcus.

"Boy, you bring your behind straight home from school and come and help me at the store."Michael said the same thing to his son daily and everyday Marcus gave the same answer.

"Yes, Sir."

It wasn't like Marcus had anywhere to go anyway because he really didn't have any friends. One of the only benefits of Michael's treatment of Marcus was that he encouraged him to workout. Being that the only thing he was allowed to do was work, study and workout, his body and his mind were showing the results of that. Marcus was about to graduate at the top of his class and his body was the topic of discussion amongst the ladies of Caldwell High School. As Marcus walked to school he was reminded of his mother and brother because he had to stare at the man who killed them.

*WILLIAM J. REEVES FOR SHERIFF*

The billboard read along with a big picture of the man himself. It was unfathomable that a man could go from killing his mother and brother and walking away unharmed, to running for sheriff. But Marcus was not the only one who had to deal with seeing William Reeves smug face every day. His dad had to see him too, but he did not deal with it as well as Marcus, he pushed himself further and further in his whole hiding from the world.

"You are late, Mr. Tanner." Marcus looked up to see vice principal Sledge staring at him giving him her look of death. Marcus tried to think of an excuse but before he could she said,

"No need for excuses Marcus, just *try* to make it to school on time. You are class Valedictorian after all." This was the first time he had heard this, and he was pleased beyond words.

"Thank you, Ms. Sledge."

She waved him off. "No need for that, you earned it. And I know that it has not been easy on you…" she said letting her words trail off.

All of Marcus's teachers knew what he had been through, as well as his home situation.

"You hurry off to class." Ms. Sledge said and watched him walk to class.

It was a normal day for Marcus that was until he made it home from school. The first thing that he noticed when he got home was that his father was there. His father was usually at work at the store while Marcus was at school. Marcus saw his father's truck outside, and he could hear him moving around upstairs.

"Dad I'm going to grab a snack and then head on down to the store!"

Marcus waited for a reply but got none, so he headed to the kitchen and made a peanut butter and jelly sandwich. Right as he sat down at the table to eat his snack his father appeared in the kitchen.

"Marcus, I want you to take a walk with me."

As soon as his father said this he was headed out the backdoor. Marcus had to jog to catch up with his father as he darted through the woods. Marcus used to play in these same woods when he was young but not since Mikey died. Michal led Marcus to a clearing in the woods and stopped.

"What I am about to tell you is not to be shared with anyone else." His father said to make eye contact with him.

"Yes, sir." And with that Michael kneeled and found a handle that was buried under pine needles and pulled. A door appeared in the ground with a pair of steps heading down. Michael descended the stairs and Marcus followed. His father felt in the dark for a string suspended from a light fixture. He pulled it and now the darkness was filled with light.

The space was filled with pictures of Mikey and his mother also with pictures of the man responsible for killing them."I know that I have not been the most loving or nurturing parent, but I did what I thought was necessary for what is to come." Michael stated cryptically.

Marcus looked at his father full of questions because he did not know where all of this was leading.

"When your mother and brother died, I made up my mind right then that I would die too. But I would die killing the man that killed them and anyone of his buddies who stood in my way. But I had another responsibility to tend to before that could be accomplished. YOU. I owed it to your mother and brother to raise you to be a good man who could carry on the family name and move beyond that tragic day. But because I had to wait until you were old enough to take care of yourself, the man who tore our family apart has grown to be quite powerful."

Marcus gazed around the room and there were pictures of William Reeves scattered all around the room. It showed him at work. There were pictures of him in his driveway getting in the car. There were pictures of him with a woman and two kids that Marcus could only assume was his family. But there were other pictures as well like the ones outside of seedy hotels in the company of women who were not his wife. It was clear to Marcus that his father was stalking Reeves with the intentions of killing him.

"The time has come Marcus." The words hung in the air.

"Dad, I don't understand. I mean I can't..." Marcus struggled to find the right words.

"Son, I love you. Just as I loved your mother and brother. This is something that must be done." The way that Michael said it left no room for debate, so Marcus was quiet as his father spoke.

"I know that this is a lot for you to deal with right now, but I know the man that I raised knows that deep down inside this is what must be done. No matter what people say about me after I am gone, I want you to think about what happened that day and how you felt and I want you to judge me on that!"

Michael said looking his son in the eye. Marcus began to cry and his father hugged him and said,

"Don't cry son lord knows I have done enough of that for the both of us."Michael grabbed a heavy duffel bag and the two of them left the bunker and returned to the house. Once they were seated at the kitchen table his dad said, "No matter what you decide to do with the house when I am gone, do me a favor and keep my little sanctuary intact.

Marcus only nodded

"Dad let me ask you, when did you build that?

"As soon as I knew what I had to do. Son in my mind it is war! And back when I was in the war, we had bunkers like that so it just seemed right to me."

In a strange way it made sense to Marcus as well.

"I made plans for you to stay with your grandfather until you go away to school." Michael stated.

Michael's mom had passed away the previous summer from liver cancer and now it was just his dad. Later on that night Marcus could not sleep. He was thinking about everything that his father shared with him that day. He honestly did not know what to think or feel in a situation like this.

When the sun finally rose Marcus went to his closet to get dressed but his clothes were not there. He looked on his dresser and there was a note. It read.


*Dear Son,*

*I never told you how proud of you I am. I could not have asked for a better son than you Marcus. I wish that I could be there to watch you grow into manhood and see what kind of life you make for yourself. I just want you to be happy and never forget the lessons that I taught you. There is no need for you to go to the store today or any other day because I sold it. The money is in an account for you. The house and all the land that surrounds it now belongs to you as well. When you get out of school today your grandfather will be there to pick you up. I love you please try to remember that.*

*Your Father*

Marcus did not realize it but by the time he was finished reading the letter his cheeks were wet with tears. Marcus did as he was told and went to school, but it was as if he was in a haze all day long. He was in his sixth period math class when Ms. Sledge came to the door. She motioned for his teacher Mr. Bell to step out into the hall

Marcus watched as Ms. Sledge told Mr. Bell something that must have been horrible because his hand flew to his mouth and he pleaded with shock.

Mr. Bell looked as if he had trouble standing but he made his way back into the classroom. He made eye contact with Marcus who was staring at him from the time that he walked in.

"Um, Marcus? Ms. Sledge needs to speak with you." Marcus did not ask any questions. He did not need to ask any questions; he knew exactly what was going on right now. Marcus was led into the office where to his surprise his grandfather was sitting there, waiting.

Ms. Sledge to her credit did not try to beat around the bush she got right down to it.

"Marcus, I don't know how to tell you this other than just to say it. Marcus, your father was killed this morning."

Michael had been sitting a few houses away from Reeves's house since four am. Even though he knew that no one left the house until seven am. He had the Reeves's family routine down. His wife Shelly would take one child to school and the other to day care, before going for her shift at the hospital where she was a nurse. The hospital is where her and her husband met after the car crash that changed Michael's life forever.

Reeves usually left the house about 7:45am every day and right now it was 7:43. Michael had to time this just right. He moved the car up a few feet until he was parked in front of William's next-door neighbor's house. He did not want to give Reeves any time to react in case he happened to be looking out the window. He walked calmly up to Reeves' neighbor's house as far as the front porch and then cut across the lawn until he was right on the side of Reeves' house. As soon as he was in position, the front door of Reeves's house opened and there he was. Drinking a cup of coffee and holding the morning paper under his arm. He turned to his right to wave at Hal Daniels who lived across the street. William thought to himself that Hal had a strange look on his face.``Must be drinking again." Reeves said to himself. Hal was waving his arms frantically as Reeves tried to make out what he was saying.

"Hal, I can't hear you." Reeves said but Hal was running and pointing at something. When it finally dawned him what Hal was saying it was too late.

"LOOK OUT!" Was what Hal was saying.

Reeves dropped his coffee and paper and tried to go for his weapon but was not fast enough. Michael walked to the bottom of the stairs and opened fire with the shotgun catching Reeves in the middle of his chest. The force of the blast knocked Reeves off his feet and back into the house. The quiet cul-de-sac that Reeves called home was turned into a war zone with the booming blast of the shotgun. Michael went up the stairs to the front door, he could see into the foyer. He prepared to kill Reeves if he was not already dead.

When he stepped inside not only was Reeves not dead he was nowhere in sight. Before Michael could react he heard two things that made him spring into action. One was the sound of gunfire coming from the kitchen. The other was police sirens in the distance. Reeves and Michael exchanged gunfire in the cramped confines of the house. Reeves was in bad shape but not as bad as he could have been thanks to his bullet proof vest. Reeves had no time to think who this could have been coming to his home to kill him, but he didn't have to.

"You killed my family, you murdering bastard!" Michael said through the thick haze of gun smoke.

"Too bad I ain't kill you too boy!" Reeves responded knowing full well who it was now. "And that nigger child that was with you in the wreck!"

At the mention of his boy Michael threw all caution to the wind and stepped into the open and fired as he walked toward Reeves' position. He blew holes through the wall as Reeves tried to scramble for cover. He squeezed the trigger until nothing came out and then dropped the shotgun and grabbed his sidearm a 45. Ruger. In the lull in the action they both heard the same thing at the same time. The sirens were close. Very close!

"You hear that boy? The Cavalry's here!" Reeves knew he had to buy some time until he could get some back up here to assist him. "Listen, why don't you just give up?" Reeves said crouched down on the side of the island in the kitchen, Reeves waited and when he did not get a response, he risked a peek over the counter and saw nothing. Michael was gone.

Michael knew he did not have long to make it out of the area before it would be swarming with police. Michael had no way of knowing this, but Hal saw him when he pulled to the house and watched everything. He called the police and reported a suspicious man in the area. But he called again when he saw the gunfire and reported a police officer in danger. And now the entire police force was dispatched. Michael was doing 70 miles an hour in a residential area and he made a right turn down a quiet block. The police were headed up that same block in the opposite direction.

As soon as they saw each other they knew that the chase was on. The police car made a wild U-turn and began to give chase.

Michael had no intention of letting them take him alive, so he floored it in his bid for escape.

But the police radioed that they were in pursuit of the likely perpetrator in the attempted murder of a police officer and they soon joined in the chase as well. Everywhere that Michael thought to turn there was a police car there. He looked up into the air and saw that he was being pursued from there as well by a police helicopter. Michael made an attempt to get on to the interstate but as soon as he did, he quickly realized his mistake. There were roadblocks set up on every ramp. Michael stopped the car for a second as the police at the roadblock leaned over their car hoods and trunks with guns all pointed at him. Cars that had been chasing him now pulled up and sealed him in from behind. He was caught and he knew it. It was only one thing left to do now. Go and join his wife and son, Andréa and Mikey. "I will be there to join you soon. God please, watch over Marcus. Do not let the decisions that I made here today effect and make it any harder than it has already been." And with that said Michael got out of the driver seat of the car and opened fire on the police.

# CHAPTER 3

PRESENT DAY

"We need to make the murder of our police officers a federal offense. And those who are caught should be tried and put to death!"

Marcus was watching CNN and that was what one of the many analysts had to say on the subject. The camera cut away to a live feed from Cleveland, Ohio and it was a protest rally going on and the reporter on the scene was talking to one of the organizers of the event. His name was Shawn Butler.

"It has been reported that this event is in support of the serial cop killer known as the POPE. Is that correct Mr. Butler?"

"This event is about us rallying around a brother that is not afraid to take a stand for what he thinks is right." was his quick reply.

"But do you think that it is right for him to be hunting down and killing police officers?"

"What is not right is this epidemic of murders of unarmed citizens all across the country, but it has happened time and time again. So, to answer your question is it right? Maybe not but unfortunately it is what is necessary!"

"Do you and your followers think all police are bad?"

"No, we do not. I understand that the police have a very tough and important job to do and that they are a very important part of society. I don't think that all of them are bad, but I do know that they are taught to have their brother officers' back no matter what! So that is what we are out here doing today, we are having our brother's back!"

Before the segment ended Marcus saw how big the crowd was and they were all wearing t-shirts with *The POPE* on them. It was enough to almost bring Marcus to tears. The rally he just watched was not something that was going on in just Ohio. Similar events were being held in major cities around the country. This is not what Marcus expected when he started all of this, but it was happening. Marcus had set up numerous social media accounts that he used to post messages out to the world. And the people had responded. He had over a million followers on every site.

His followers had even made their own page dedicated to the POPE. Marcus was so inspired by what he had just seen on the news that he had to send a message out to the world. Marcus set up his camera and sat down with a black banner that had the POPE spelled in white letters. He put on a black hood that looked like the executioner's mask from the middle ages. He began by saying,

"Today I see brothers and sisters out in the streets supporting me and saying to the oppression and the oppressors 'NO MORE!' I will live my life until my last breath fighting for you. I only hope that I can inspire you the way that you have inspired me. And together we can inspire more to fight for themselves." Marcus uploaded his short message and watched as the world listened to what he had to say. He read all of the comments. It was black and white. People who loved him as well as those that hated him. It was Christians, Jews, and Muslims. It was people from all around the world.

*The POPE* had become a movement.


### MEANWHILE

Agent Marrow was home watching the same CNN news report as the man she was trying to catch. It boggled her mind how so many people could believe in such a low life scumbag, she paid close attention to all of the social media sites and she was even listed as one of his followers. Under a fake name of course. Marrow read the post from the deranged fuck she thought to herself. Reading his latest post got her so mad that she wanted to throw her phone against the wall. She decided what she needed was a long hot bath. It had been ages since she had time to just sit and soak in a hot bath. As soon as she began to run the water the phone rang. She answered on the third ring.

"This had better be good!"

"Grab your overnight bag. Our guy is at it again."

*NEWARK, NEW JERSEY*

"Couldn't this guy find a nicer city to kill a cop in?" Agent Connolly said looking around at the decrepit buildings and people who looked like they just came from a Walking Dead casting call. The crime scene was swarming with cops, state, local and federal officials. The media was there as well.

"A POPE murder is the hottest ticket in town I see." Marrow replied looking at the media circus. Marrow put those thoughts out of her mind and focused on the crime scene. "This is not our guy." She said in a matter of fact manner.

"What do you mean? How could you be so sure?"

"Well for starters unless our guy is all of a sudden not an expert shot, which needed to spray an excessive number of rounds to hit his target. I don't think so. Remember what happened in San Diego? Four cops, minimal shots fired! And those guys were shooting back! No this is something different." Agent Marrow said, shaking her head.

She looked into the car and it was two officers that looked like they didn't know what hit them. From what they knew the police received a call about a domestic disturbance. The dispatcher said the call came at 10:02pm. The address given was to the abandoned house that the cop car was parked in front of.

"From the amount of shell casing found on the side of the house it looked like the shooter laid in wait in the alley." Marrow started pointing at the house. "And when they pulled up bam!" As Marrow was speaking Connolly had his phone out looking online.

"Bingo!" Connolly said, handing his phone over to his partner.

*"Tonight Jersey put on for the POPE."* The post read.

It was someone taking credit who was clearly not the POPE. Marrow continued reading. There were a bunch of different comments in response to the post saying how they" ripped" the POPE better in their respective hometowns.

"Oh my God!"

Marrow said with her mouth hanging wide open. We are about to have copycat shooters all around the country.

After leaving the latest crime scene Agents Marrow and Connolly were at the New York field office of the FBI.

"We have to get ahead of this thing before it is beyond our control." Marrow said, trying to figure out a way to do just that. "We are already running all around the country trying to figure out way to catch this fucking POPE guy, now we have hundreds maybe even thousands of his little disciples to deal with?"

"And just when you thought it couldn't get any worse, it does just that!"Connolly said, shaking his head.

The two Agents stopped talking as a group of people entered the office.

The woman who was clearly in charge stopped short in front of the office door of the Special Agent in charge. When he saw who was at his door, he went out of his way to let her know that he would give his total cooperation. After a brief chat he said, "Listen up everybody, "she quieted him with a raise of her hand and said.

"My name is Alicia Baisley and I am from the Office of Homeland Security. I will be working with you on catching the man we have come to know as the POPE."

## SEVERAL YEARS EARLIER

"Chug, Chug, Chug, Chug!!"

The crowded room cheered in unison. College life was everything they said it would be. And Marcus hated every minute of it. It seemed to him like he was the only adult in a room full of children. The frat party that Marcus was at had been trying to get him to pledge since he was a freshman and now that he was a junior, nothing he saw changed his mind.

"Wild party huh Marky Mark?"

Asked a guy named Kevin Biglin who everyone called Biglin. Marcus thought it was because it was fun just to say Biglin. He also insisted on calling Marcus "Marky Mark" no matter how many times he tried to correct him.

"Yeah it's a wild party." Marcus said wishing he could be anywhere but there.

"Hey Marcus, when are you going to dance with me?"Asked a girl named Patricia who everyone called Patsy.

"Not right now I'm not feeling too good Patsy."

And that was the wrong thing to say to a girl that was pre-med and had the hots for you.

"Why don't you let me come back to your dorm and take care of you then?" She said batting her eyes. The way she was looking in her short skirt and tight sweater made Marcus consider it but quickly pushed the thought from his mind. He could tell that she was the clingy type. That was the last thing Marcus wanted. Growing up he was forced to be a loner and now it was the only way that he knew how to live, and it was fine with him.

Marcus stayed at the party a while longer and then decided to call it a night. As he was walking to his car, he saw a girl on the side of the road. Actually, two girls on the side of the road. One of them was completely passed out. The other tried to wake her but her attempts were in vain. Being that they were directly in front of his car it was no way that he could pull off without offering some kind of assistance.

"Nicky, wake up!" Stated the girl who was trying to wake her friend up."Come on Nicky get up!" And lightly slapped her face. And to this Nicky responded by letting out a loud wet sounding fart. "It looks like you two could use a hand." The girl heard a voice say and turned around and saw Marcus standing there holding his nose.

"I am so embarrassed!" The girl said because of her friend, who was still totally out of it.

"You want me to carry her to your car so that you can drive her home?" The girl looked down and shook her head.

"I can't drive! She was supposed to be MY ride home!" At this revelation Marcus could not help but laugh.

"It's not funny!" The girl said getting upset, but then realized quickly just how comical her situation was and could not help but laugh herself.

"I wouldn't be able to sleep tonight if I didn't at least offer you a ride home."The girl thought about it and came to the conclusion that she did in fact need some help. Marcus kneeled and scooped the young woman off the ground like she weighed nothing at all. He laid her on the backseat of his car. After getting her settled in he opened the door for her friend. Once in the driver's seat he said, "Where to?"

She gave him the address of a house that was only a few miles from campus.

"Looks like your friend really had a great time tonight." Marcus said gesturing toward the backseat.

"That's not how she usually is but her and her boyfriend just broke up and she has been going through a rough time lately." Marcus stopped at a red light and for the first time really noticed how pretty his passenger was. She had shoulder length blonde hair; with the bluest eyes he had ever seen. But what he really liked about her were her lips. She had a full mouth with lips that were made for kissing. As they pulled onto her block she said to Marcus,

"I want to thank you for being such a gentleman tonight. If you hadn't come along, I don't know what we would have done."

"Don't mention it I was just doing what I thought was the right thing."

"Come on, Nicky, we're home." The girl said to her friend who was now snoring loudly. She tried to wake her up a few more times with negative results.

Marcus decided to take over. He reached into the back seat and took her out and picked her up and carried her to the front steps of the house. The girl opened the door and said,

"I hate to tell you this, but we live on the third floor."

"Well good thing that she is not heavy." Marcus said and proceeded up the stairs. He made it as far as between the second and third floor when he felt the girl in his arms wake up and miserably admitted,

"I think I am going to be sick!"

Right before she threw up all over Marcus and herself.

"Oh my God I'm so sorry the girl said this to her friend who for all intents and purposes looked as if she passed out again and was oblivious to the mess that she made. Marcus just wanted to get upstairs and get out of there as fast as he could. He made it to the apartment where he was led to a bedroom where he quickly dumped the drunken girl on the bed and was on his way.

"Hey, wait up a minute." The girl said. "I feel terrible for what just happened. I can't have you drive all the way home with that crap all over you. I have a washer and dryer in the back. I can have you cleaned up in a couple of minutes." She saw the look of hesitation on his face and said, "And I won't take no for an answer."

And with that Marcus unbuttoned the flannel shirt he was wearing and took off the t-shirt he was wearing underneath and gave them to the girl who quickly put them in the wash. She came back and went into the room with her friend and got her dressed for bed and came back and joined Marcus who was seated in the living room. "I noticed some of the books that you have. Let me guess you are majoring in criminal justice?" Marcus asked her.

"As a matter of fact, I am. How did you know that?"

"I have those same books because I have a double major in criminal justice and engineering."

"Oh, so you're like some kind of genius huh?" She asked playfully.

"Nah not at all I am only pursuing what interests me. Speaking of which, what is your name anyway?"

She smiled and said, "My name is Alicia, Alicia Baisley. And besides being tall, dark and handsome, you are?"

"My name is Marcus Tanner." He responded with a charming smile.

## *A FEW MONTHS LATER*

Since the night that Marcus and Alicia met, they had become inseparable. Marcus walked into the library where he saw Alicia with a pile of books surrounding her. He crept up behind her and kissed her on her neck. She looked up at him and smiled.

"You look happy to see me." Marcus kidded as he sat down and took his jacket off.

"You already know that I am, and I need to take a break anyway. What better way to do it then with the love of my life."

"Well that's good because I have a surprise for you back at your place." Marcus said with a sly look on his face.

"What are you up to Mr. Tanner?"

Alicia said with her stunningly blue eyes shimmering in the light.

"You will find out later." Marcus said to her as he got up to leave. He left her to continue her studying and as he was walking out of the door of the library, he made the mistake of bumping into Jason Ballard.

"You better watch where the hell you going, BOY!" Jason sneered in his southern drawl.

"I apologize for bumping into you but the next time you call me 'BOY' I will do more than bump into you." Marcus stated calmly. So calm in fact that the two guys with Jason thought he must have a gun or he was crazy." Man this dude ain't even ain't even worth it." Jason's friend said as he led him away.

It was a few people on campus who did not approve of the fact he was dating Alicia simply based on the fact that he was black and she was white. And Jason was at the very top of that list, and he happened to be a little bit more vocal about then everyone else.

## LATER THAT NIGHT

"Babe you here?" Alicia asked as she walked into her apartment.

She knew that Marcus was there because she saw his car outside. But she did not see him until she walked into her bedroom.

She was totally blown away by what she saw. Marcus was impeccably dressed in a tailored suit that hung off his chiseled physique perfectly. There were candles and rose petals around the room.

"Marcus what's going on?"

Marcus came to her and put his hand on her chin and lifted her head so her eyes met.

"I am in love with you and I want the whole world to know it. I want to take you out and do something special with you."Alicia looked on the bed and saw a dress.

"I took the liberty of finding out your dress size. I went out and picked this up for you. I hope you like it."

"Oh, Marcus this is beautiful, I love it!" Marcus led her to the bathroom where he had already had her bath water drawn and he waited while she got ready. Once she was ready, they went outside where Marcus had yet another surprise waiting for her. It was a limousine for the two of them and the driver was standing with the door open.

"Your chariot awaits." Marcus said.

They went to the best restaurant in town. Marcus had been planning this night for weeks and it had taken him that long to get the reservations.

Once they were seated and had placed their orders Alicia said, "I cannot believe you did all of this! This is turning out to be the best night of my life."

Later on as Marcus and Alicia lay in each other's arms after making love for the third time that night, Marcus said,

"You know that I love you more than anything in the world, right?"

Alicia sensing something in his tone rolled over to face him and look in his eyes.

"Yes, I know." She said feeling that he had something more to say.

"You are the person I believe I was meant to share my life with. And I can't share just the good and not the bad."

She nodded her head not knowing where all of this was headed.

"When I was ten years old my mom and my little brother Mikey were killed in a car crash. The man behind the wheel of the car that killed him was a Virginia state trooper and he was speeding and ran a light which caused the accident. But the facts of the situation had nothing to do with what happened in the aftermath. May father was dragged away from his family who lay dead in the street and was savagely beaten right in front of my eyes…"Marcus said becoming emotional." I honestly believe that the only reason that he did not die that day is because I ran and got on top of him to help. After the beating he was arrested and charged with the death of my mother and brother along with assault on the cop who killed them. He ended up beating the charges, but he was never the same after that. He told me that he had to get me ready to be a Man, a Black MAN in America. He taught me never to trust the cops. He taught me that there was no justice for black and brown people. When I was seventeen he told me that he was going to kill the man who killed my family. He died instead. My father had no love for the government, more specifically the police. Even though he never said this, I don't think he trusted white people in general. I never understood what my father was teaching me but I am starting too. I have to live my life the way I want and love who I choose to and I choose to love you."This was the first time Marcus ever put any of this into words.

"After a lifetime of pain I just want to be happy…is that asking too much?" Marcus said on the verge of tears.

"Not at all Mr. Tanner. As a matter of fact, I think I can do something that will make you a very happy man." With that she slid under the covers. As Marcus lay there enjoying the warm feeling of her mouth, he thought to himself with a smile "So this is what happiness feels like?"

## EIGHTEEN MONTHS LATER

It was graduation day and Marcus was on top of the world! Everyone was going to a big party to celebrate graduation and after the party Marcus had something that he wanted to do. He was going to ask Alicia to marry him.

"I cannot believe that we are finally out of here and on our way to the real world!" Alicia said happily.

"I can't believe it either. Just think about it, we are about to be working for one of the biggest and best police forces in the world!" Marcus said excitedly, because they had both applied and been accepted to join the LAPD.

"I have something to tell you and I don't know if you are going to like it or not. " After taking a few calming breaths Alicia got down to it.

"Remember I told you that a few people from the Department of Homeland Security had come to my class and spoke with us?" Marcus said that he did remember that. "Well what I didn't know until just now was that they were looking for recruits and my name was given to them as a potential candidate!"

Marcus could tell she was excited, and he wanted to be excited for her, but something held him back. "But the bad news is that I would have to and live in Washington."

To his credit he played it cool. "Babe that's great I am so happy for you." The ring that he held in his pocket felt like it weighed a ton right now. He did not want to ruin the night so they parted like nothing had happened but everything had changed and that was only the beginning.

"I see you still hanging out with the help Alicia." Marcus knew that voice without even having to look up. Jason Ballard.

"Jason knock it off, not tonight!"

Marcus could tell that Jason had been drinking but the way he was feeling right now it took all of his self-control to keep from putting a fist through Jason's face.

"I hear that you are about to become a LA police officer"

"You heard right."

Marcus said feeling his temper rise. Jason nodded his head up and down and said in a slurred speech.

"Well ain't that bout a bitch! First ya daddy tries to kill a police officer and got himself killed in the process and you wan-"

Before he could finish his sentence, Marcus was all over him. The first punch knocked him out cold on his feet. The rest of the punches were simply overkill.

It took almost everybody in the party to pull Marcus off Jason. When the melee was over Marcus locked eyes with Alicia and he knew that she had betrayed his trust. He was so hurt that he left school that night and never looked back.

### SEVERAL YEARS LATER

Marcus was on his first day out on patrol. He was finally a member of the LAPD; it was just a few years different.

After leaving school something in Marcus changed. He wanted to test some of the other things that his father had instilled in him. Marcus knew that his father and grandfather both served their country in war. His father told him that it was the worst mistake he had ever made. Marcus served a tour of duty in Iraq. He was on the frontline in some of the bloodiest days of the war. Roadside bombs were a major factor. At the time, he was a part of a unit that went out and found those bombs and neutralized them. In the process he had become a master of the IED or Improvised Exploding Device. Because of Marcus many service men and women are alive today. But after all the blood and carnage that he'd seen, the majority of what his father taught him was starting to sound like it had a lot of truth to it.

He once said to Marcus, "Son Uncle Sam had me thousands of miles from home killing poor and oppressed people. I did not know where I was or why I was even there." Marcus started to feel the same way. He realized that he was killing people that looked a lot like him. In time he saw that they were poor and oppressed people everywhere, just like his father taught him. Marcus only served one tour of duty because of how he started to view the war effort in Iraq.

Now he was home but from what his training officer was telling him he was still in battle.

"Don't let your guard down for a minute we are in a war zone! And THEY!" He said as he pointed his finger out the window at a crowd of men who stood in front of a liquor store. "Are enemy combatants! I just wish that we could stick 'em in Git-MO and throw away the key! But we will have to settle for Pelican Bay, ain't that right?" His training officers' name was Schaffer and he hated him from the first time he laid eyes on him.

"The second you put that uniform on you stopped being one of them and became one of us! You're not black and I ain't white! Were BLUE! And ain't nothing or nobody worse than us you hear me?"

Marcus was not paying him any mind.

"I said do you hear me?"

"Yes, sir."Marcus said, instantly reverting to the military discipline that he had received. The district where Marcus worked was a gang ridden working class area. The radio in their cruiser put out a call about a domestic disturbance nearby.

"That will be us hotshot! You ready?"

Yes, sir. I am."

And with that Schaffer played a song on his playlist. Guns and Roses "Welcome To The Jungle " This is the soundtrack to our lives right here. You watch and see."

They arrived at the location of the disturbance a short time later and it was a small crowd gathered outside of the small house. As they arrived all eyes were glued to them. For the first time since Marcus had decided to become a police officer he was nervous and doubting his decision. The people on the scene stared at them with open hostility. It was a small boy who could not have been more than eight years old in the crowd. Marcus saw him staring and decided to speak.

"How are you doing, little man?"

The young boy's reply was not at all what Marcus was expecting.

"I don't talk to cops." The crowd nodded their heads in agreement.


"We will see about that the next time Crenshaw Mafia or whatever other set y'all squabbling with this week comes through blasting." Schaffer said as they made their way to the door of the house.

A woman's voice could be heard screaming from where they were. The door was open and from where he stood Marcus could see a very large black woman and a much smaller man engaged in a heated argument."I want you to get yo shit and get the hell out!" The woman yelled.

"I ain't going no god damn where! And I advise you to stay the hell out of my damn face!"

The two went back and forth and seemed to be unaware of the police presence. Schaffer took his flashlight and knocked on the door.

"LAPD what seems to be the problem here?"

The two stopped going at each other for a second and stared at the two cops.

"Ain't no problem here, at least nothing you can help us with." The smaller man said.

"Officer I just want him out of my house, with his no good lying ass!"

"The only thing I ever lied about is when I said that I liked big women because I can't stand you fat ass!" And with that the woman lunged for the man and pinned him against the wall clawing his face.

Schaffer and Marcus attempted to intervene, but as they were pulling the woman off, the man cocked back and punched her square in the face! The punch landed on the bridge of her nose and sent blood pouring down her face.

"Did y'all see that motherfucker hit me?" She bellowed as she renewed her efforts to tear the man to pieces.

Marcus was able to move the woman far enough away so that Schaffer could handcuff the man. "What is you locking me up for, y'all seen her hit me first! I was just defending myself!"

As soon as he said this he began to struggle with Schaffer. Schaffer swept his legs from under him and soon the man was face down on the living room floor. Schaffer put his knee in his back and dropped his full weight on him. What happened next was something that would follow Marcus for the rest of his career.

"Get off of him like that!" the woman yelled and swatted Marcus to the side and charged Schaffer who still had his knee on the man's back. Luckily Marcus recovered fast and he ran after and hit her with a shoulder block just as she reached the two men and she slammed into the wall. A gigantic hole was in the wall from where she made an impact. Marcus threw her on the floor and handcuffed her.

"Ma'am you are under arrest."

By now a huge crowd had gathered at the door drawn to the loud commotion that was emanating from the house. As they hauled the two individuals to the awaiting police cruisers the rowdy crowd let them have it.

"You didn't have to do that to Thelma!" One woman shouted.

"Man, you know how these black pigs act, always trying to show out for the white cop!"Replied another man.

74

"This is Two-Charlie-Bravo requesting back up."

"What's your 20, Two-Charlie-Bravo?" Asked the dispatcher.

"2200 block of Normandy."

Marcus loaded his prisoner into the back.

"The natives are getting restless!" Schaffer jokes.

But the crowd was indeed becoming more and more volatile with every second they remained on the scene. Someone threw a bottle and out of instinct Marcus reached for his weapon.

"What are you going to do? Shoot us pig!" Said one man who looked as if he wanted to kill the both of them. But right when things looked as if there was about to be a riot, the sounds of sirens could be heard in the distance.

"You hear that? You will learn to love that sound being a cop in LA. Trust me."

The next few months were like a blur in Marcus's mind. Every day it was pretty much the same thing as the day before it. And that is that it was total chaos! Whatever fantasy Marcus had about trying to be able to make a difference from the inside went right out of the window his first month on the job.

"Let me ask you a question Rook." Rook short for rookie is what Schaffer called Marcus.

"I know you served in the war and that you made a shit load of money inventing some type of bomb detecting machine or some shit. You have a degree in engineering. Why, may I ask, do you

75

come and ride into the bowels of Hell everyday with me, when it is clear to me that you don't have to?"

Marcus could see that this was something that his training officer had given a lot of thought to, so he decided to be honest with him.

"I was raised where I was taught that the police could not and should not be trusted. As I grew up I formed my own opinion on the subject. I decided that I wanted to be an example of what I thought a policeman should be. I wanted to make a difference."As soon as the last words were out of his mouth did Schaffer slam on the breaks and bring the car to a screeching halt.

"Let me tell you something. The worst thing that you can be on this side of the law is an idealist!" He said that the last word like you would say a "pedophile". "Because your ideas may cause somebody to get killed one of these days! Let me elaborate. When you are out here on the street your only concerns are that you and your partner make it home at night! That is it! When you start thinking about other shit, shit that will make you second guess yourself and get you or the man next to you killed! If your heart's not in the right place son then do everybody a favor and turn in that shield. You served in Iraq; this is no different than that! It is us versus them! Remember that!"

After a while Marcus was paired up with his new partner. His name was Ryan Holmes. He was from Lubbock, Texas.

"Go on and drive rookie, I like to keep my eyes on the street." Holmes was an eight-year veteran on the force. "I am only pounding a beat until I get accepted into S.W.A.T. That's the whole reason I came out here from Texas in the first place."

Ryan seemed like a pretty decent guy to Marcus and they got along well. One night while out on patrol Marcus was behind the wheel as usual when a late model Chevy Impala ran a red light and Marcus decided to pull him over.

He hit the lights on his cruiser and ordered the driver to pull over. Both he and Holmes approached the car, he on the driver side with his partner on the passenger side. The car was occupied by three individuals.

"Do you know why I know why I am pulling you over?" Marcus asked the driver.

"I have no idea sir."

"It's because you blew through a red light a couple of blocks back. License and registration." The man reached into the glove compartment and retrieved the documents. The driver was a white male by the name of Steven Alcott according to his license.

"Just sit tight and I will be right back." The two officers made their way back to their car where Marcus ran his license, and wrote him a ticket. As he was writing the ticket a call went out over the radio about an apparent gang drive-by shooting and pursuit of said individuals.

"Come on Tanner let's cut these bozos loose so we can get some of that gang banger beat down!" Holmes said excitedly, a little too excited. Marcus thought to himself.

77

After writing the ticket and running his name through the system, Marcus walked back to the car. The backseat passenger turned and looked at him and they made eye contact, it was only for a brief second, but it was all that was needed to put him on edge.

He had seen that look a lot since he took this job. It was a look of uncontrolled hatred. As he walked back to the driver he also saw him looking at him through the side mirror. When he made it to the driver he looked into the backseat and could not see the passenger's hand because they were between his thigh and the door. "Hands"

Marcus shouted and Holmes looked at him as if to say, "what the hell!"

Marcus repeated his command and all hands were raised in the air.

"Out of the car now!" When the backseat passenger got out the unmistakable sound of a gun being dropped could be heard by all who were present. Holmes retrieved the weapon and all the suspects were handcuffed. Three more guns were found in the car two in the front and an assault rifle in the trunk. As it would turn out these were the perpetrators of the so-called "Gang drive-by". The victim in that shooting was set to testify against the trio in a gun running operation. When word spread around the station house about what took place Marcus was a hero. "Way to go Rook!" His sergeant complimented him. Marcus had to admit to himself he was proud of what he did.

After work, some of the guys invited Marcus out to go and get some drinks.

"Let me get a round of drinks for the rookie who popped his cherry tonight!" An older cop named Sanders said loud enough for everyone to hear.

"Hey Holmes, I heard while the rook was kicking ass and taking names you were somewhere scared shitless!" Chimed in a detective named Mendez.

"Fuck you Mendez!" Holmes spat.

Not paying Holmes any attention the detective continued to berate him.

"That's why your partner put in his paperwork to be reassigned because you are nothing but a big pussy!" Everyone laughed and joined in the fun "They say that everything is bigger in Texas!" Said an officer named James through fits of laughter.

Marcus felt bad for his partner and all the abuse that he was taking.

"Come on guys take it easy."

He said he was trying to ease his partner's suffering. The night went on and Marcus had a good time and felt like this was the first step in bonding with his fellow officers.

The next day when he arrived for his shift Holmes looked as if he was in a foul mood.

"You alright partner?" Marcus inquired as they put away their gear and climbed into the car.

"I'm fine. Let's get to work."

Their shift was going smoothly. When they saw something that caught both of their attention.

"Did you see that?" Holmes asked as Marcus was already turning the car around in pursuit.

The two cars had pulled alongside each other, when one car threw a large bag through the window of the other and drove in separate directions. Choosing the car that was on the receiving end of the bag, Marcus was now in hot pursuit. The car was a Challenger that was full of horsepower and it was hard for the much slower police car to keep up with. The suspects turned down a series of alleys and one-ways until Marcus had no idea where they went. It was by chance that Marcus drove past a house on a residential block and happened to spot the Challenger parked in the driveway.

"Got that fucker now!" Holmes said excitedly as he told Marcus.

"Park up the block."

"Let's call this in," Marcus said, reaching for the radio.

"NO! "Holmes said, knocking his hand off the radio. "Let's just take a look first and see what we come up with."Holmes said as he got out and made his way toward the house.

Being that it was already dark outside they stayed in the shadows and crept to a window on the side of the house. The first window they looked in was the living room, which was empty but they could see a male Hispanic walking into the kitchen. Holmes moved toward the kitchen window where he saw another man empty the contents of the bag onto a table. It was at least a kilo of black tar heroin.

"Can we call it in now?" Marcus asked.

Holmes shook his head and said,

"No time, we have to get them now before it is too late."

This did not make sense to Marcus but being that Holmes was the senior officer he went along with him. Holmes went to the backdoor.

"One, two, three!"

And he kicked the backdoor open and caught both of them completely off guard.

"Freeze LAPD!"

Holmes shouted with his weapon drawn. The man who was sitting at the table with the heroin took the contents of the bag and threw them at Holmes in an effort to get away. Meanwhile the other suspect attempted to flee through the house. Marcus went after the second suspect and tackled him in the living room and quickly subdued him. Marcus returned to the kitchen where he heard a scuffle and was amazed to see Holmes on the ground with the suspect on top of him. Marcus drew his nightstick and caught the perp on the side of the head. He fell to the floor unconscious.

"Partner, you ok?" Marcus asked.

Holmes waved him off.

"Yeah I'm alright."

But he sure did not look like it in Marcus's opinion, but he decided to leave it alone. Once Holmes recovered, he started to look around the house. Holmes found not only weapons and drugs but cash. A lot of cash!

"Can we call this in now?" Marcus asked, starting to get annoyed by the whole situation.

"Right after we split this up." Holmes said going through the large stacks of cash and dividing it into large stacks.

"I don't know about this." Marcus responded, not wanting to have anything to do with stealing money from a crime scene.

"Man look what that fucker did to my face!" Holmes said pointing to the suspect that was still unconscious.

"This is for my pain and suffering."

"Well you can take what you want, I didn't see anything."

Marcus said and went to grab his prisoner and put him in the car. While in the car he called in the arrest that was made. When the backup units and an ambulance were called to look at the cuts and bruises Holmes had sustained in the fight. When Marcus returned to the station and was preparing to write his report when Holmes wandered over and sat down.

"You got that we were in hot pursuit all the way to the house and never lost sight of them right?" Marcus said nothing and just looked at him. "And they ran in the house and we ran right after them right?" Again, Marcus said nothing. "And the only money that was recovered was what we put into evidence right?"

Marcus did not like that he was being asked to lie. He did not like that he was asked to be exactly like the one his father warned him about. But he still found himself saying,

"Yeah partner I got you."

As the months wore on Marcus became disenchanted with life on the force.

Day in and day out he found himself locking up people who were already down on the bottom. More and more he could hear his father's voice saying, "They are already poor and oppressed people and the government sends in the cops to keep them in line." He didn't want to believe his father was right all of these years but he had a front row seat to the truth every day.

And to make matters worse him and Holmes were not on the same page at all!

Marcus felt like Holmes had something to prove and he would do it at any cost.

Marcus didn't know what went down with Holmes and his old partner but whatever it was it had to be bad because a lot of officers they worked with called him a coward and whole lot worse behind his back.

While working one night during the middle of the shift, Marcus and Holmes decided to stop and get a bite to eat. They went to a taco stand and placed their orders.

"I hope I run across that piece of shit that did that to Sanchez." Holmes replied

It was a Be On the Lookout for a young black kid wearing a backpack that got into a scuffle with a young officer named Sanchez. In the ensuing fight the kid pushed Sanchez into oncoming traffic and he was struck by a car.

Marcus was about to answer when out of the corner he saw something that made him stop. It was a group of young black men and women ordering tacos and the look that they gave the two officers said it all. In the preceding months there had been an uptick in police related shootings. Marcus followed them closely in the news and he was as upset as anyone else. But what made him the most upset is that time after time the police officers got off the hook! This made him think of his family. He thought of his little brother Mikey. He thought of his mom. And he thought of his dad. Those thoughts made him lose his appetite.

"You are not hungry, partner?" Holmes asked, eyeing his uneaten taco.

"Nah here you go." A short time later they were back on patrol when Holmes said,

"Damn it's a slow night."

Marcus thought about it and said,

"I will take a slow night any night. That means less paperwork for me!"

"Not me I need some action! Matter of fact let's go through the projects."

Holmes said with a devilish look on his face. The projects in question were notorious for gun violence and drug activity. It was almost a certainty that they would find the action that Holmes so desperately desired over there.

"You have got to be kidding me."

Marcus said ready to veto the idea.

"Come on bro!" Holmes said, sounding like a big kid.

Against his better judgment Marcus relented.

"But you're doing all of the paperwork."

On the drive over Holmes was looking out of the window and he saw something that made him say "Pull over Now!"

Marcus did as he was told and soon saw what made him say that. It was a young black male about six feet tall wearing a backpack.

"Hands on the car homeboy!" Holmes ordered the young man.

"For what? I ain't do shit. What y'all messing with me for?" Marcus saw that the young man was wearing a uniform from a well-known fast food chain and asked

"Where are you coming from?"

Sensing that Marcus was less an asshole than his partner, the young man replied.

"I just got off of work and I am walking to the bus stop."

Marcus believed his story and said, "You got any I.D on you?"

The man replied that he did and handed it to Marcus.

"I am about to go and run your name, if you don't have any warrants you will be on your way shortly. So cool out and keep my partner company."

Holmes was livid that he didn't get the chance to fuck with the kid a little bit, even if wasn't the guy that they were looking for. Marcus was in the car giving the information to the dispatcher when he looked up and saw the two of them staring at each other.

"You better be glad my partner saved your little ass!" "Man I ain't worried about you, you're just another scared ass white boy with a gun and a badge!" The younger man said and started to laugh.

This simple act enraged Holmes. It was bad enough that he had guys on the job laughing at him and calling him a coward but he be damned if he was going to take it from this punk! Marcus was waiting for confirmation when he looked and saw the kid take his backpack off of one shoulder. At that moment the dispatcher came back on the line and said all was clear. Then he heard Holmes say, "Stop! Don't move!"

The next thing he saw was an image that would haunt him for the rest of his life. Officer Holmes pulled his weapon and shot the man in the face. The instant the gun went off Marcus was out of the car and in Holmes' face yelling.

"What the fuck did you just do? Why the fuck would you shoot him?" Marcus was irate.

"He made a move! He went inside his book bag I thought he was going for a gun!"

Marcus looked at his bag which was by his side and still zipped up."

You saw him take his bag OFF, not go INSIDE!" Marcus said looking at the man whose wide open lifeless eyes stared at him.

"You killed an innocent man."

Marcus could see the headlines. He could not believe that he was in the middle of a shooting of an unarmed civilian. The gravity of his actions must have caught up to Holmes because he said,

"I can't go down for this! With my history they will prosecute me and send me to jail for the rest of my life!"

Marcus was not paying him any attention; he was too consumed with his own thoughts.

"You have to help me partner!" Were the words that snapped Marcus out of his daze.

"What did you say?"

Holmes began to stutter "Yo-yo you have to help me! Look we can use this!" Holmes said as he ran to the trunk and went into his bag where he stored his gear and grabbed a gun. He held it out for Marcus to see.

"We could say he had this!" Holmes said as he kneeled down and put the gun into the dead man's hand. It was like Marcus was outside of his body looking at himself as if he didn't have anything to do with what was taking place. He looked at the young man and then he looked at his partner whose eyes were pleading for help. Then back to the dead man and he walked over to the man kneeled beside him and said, "I am truly sorry." Then he took the 380.automatic out of his hand, stood up and shot Holmes in the head.

# CHAPTER 4

"We just want to know what happened. That is all we are here to do today."

Stated the internal affairs officer Nathan Spivey, who was accompanied by another officer named Teresa Macklin.

"Just start at the beginning and walk us through your night that evening."

Marcus sat next to the lawyer that was sent in by the police union to help him through his interview.

"It all happened so fast." He began. He took a deep breath to calm himself and began to tell his story.

"We were out on patrol and we saw a kid who Holmes thought could be the BOLO we were keeping an eye out for who was involved in an assault on a police officer."

"That would be the officer Fernando Sanchez?" Macklin asked.

"Yes. We stopped the young man and asked for identification. We detained him while I ran his name through the system for warrants. While I was in my squad car, I could see Dunn reaching for something. Holmes saw it too but he was too late….."Marcus stopped appearing to be overcome with emotions." The kid drew a silver gun. It looked to be a 380. Auto and fired one round that struck Holmes but not before he returned fire."No one said anything for a few minutes while they digested the information they just received.

"What do you think you could have done differently if anything, that could have changed the tragic outcome of this tragic incident?"Internal Affairs Officer Spivey asked offhandedly.

But before Marcus could answer, his attorney put his hand over his hand.

"Don't answer that!" He then shot Spivey a look that could have melted steel.

"Don't you think for one second that you can twist this in any way to make Marcus look bad on this? This man just lost his partner and there nothing he could have done about it, Period! So you can cut the crap right now!"

"Calm down Larry."

It was Teresa Macklin.

"We are just doing our job. You know as well as anyone that we have to ask these questions before anyone else does. Alright this concludes our interview for now. Marcus we will be in touch with you. You take care of yourself alright?" Macklin said as she gathered her things and left.

As Marcus left the station house the media was in a feeding frenzy! And the angry crowd wanted whoever was involved to pay. The murdered boy's name was Tyrone Dunn and he was 19yearsold. By all accounts he was a very good young man.

Marcus was taken home by his lawyer in the back of a tinted town car. As he drove by the angry crowd and who yelled for justice and screamed for the officer to pay for what he had done.

Later that night Marcus was alone in his condo. He was trying his best to process the event of the past few hours. He watched as his partner killed an unarmed man. Then he killed his partner for killing the unarmed man. Then he lied to the man. The INNOCENT unarmed man. It was almost too much for him to handle. Marcus started to think of his father. He thought about how his father always tried to warn him about the police and how some of them did not know how to handle the power that was put into their hands. Thinking of his father made him think of how he lived and ultimately died. It made him think about his own life and legacy. In his attempts to cover the truth, Marcus lied to that innocent young man! He would forever be known as a cop killer! No, Marcus could not and would not allow that to happen.

"I am no better than all those other cops who killed innocent people and got away with it." He thought to himself.

The entire night he wrestled with the idea of turning himself in and paying the price for his actions. But he would pay for killing Holmes not for the young man who deserved justice. As he was lost in thought he glanced at the TV screen and saw the brother of Tyrone Dunn speaking to the media.

"My brother was the most peaceful and fun-loving person I have ever had the pleasure of meeting. There is nothing anyone could tell me to make me think otherwise. I had nineteen great years of being his brother and I think I know him better than anyone. My brother hated guns. My brother hated how some black men in America glorified the wrong things. My brother would never hurt anybody, period! I know right now I sound just like every other grieving family member across this scarred country. But the difference is I know my brother was innocent! I am speaking to the man who took my brother away from this world. You took away a man who would have made a difference one day. What difference are you prepared to make?"

The camera cut away to the anchor in the studio but by that time Marcus was no longer listening. The words that he just heard had found their mark. Marcus knew that he did not kill Tyrone Dunn, but he did kill his reputation. Because of him the world would now think of him as a cop killer. Earlier in the night his lawyer called him a hero. But he was no hero. Not even close, at least…not yet.

### SEVENTEEN MONTHS LATER

It was a crisp fall night two days before Halloween. Marcus was parked in the parking lot of Home Depot looking into the small screen that he held in his lap. The drone that hovered over the target's location could not be seen but that was the whole point. Just like clockwork the blue Chrysler 300 pulled into the driveway and the driver got out. Marcus watched from his bird's eye view of the man he was tracking that night. His name was Aaron Bond.

He was a Cincinnati police officer. And right now, he was on administrative leave for an "incident" in which a young mother and her child lost their lives. Bond was on duty when he saw a woman drive by his squad car while talking on her cell phone. Bond initiated a traffic stop and signaled the woman to pull over. She did as she was ordered. When Bond got to the car, he could see that she was frantic. She continued to talk to someone on the phone even though officer Bond ordered her off the phone. As it turns out the young woman a 25-year-old named Shantae Bridges was on the phone with her babysitter. Her son had eaten some shrimps and was having an allergic reaction. Shantae did not eat shrimp and she never fed them to him. So she had no idea he was allergic to them. But right now, he was gasping for air as his throat swelled shut and cut off his air supply. Shantae's newborn baby was in the back in a car seat and was crying. Officer Bond continued to tell her to get off of the phone as she tried to talk to the babysitter. She pleaded with him for help. He told her one last time "get off of the phone or else."Shantae pleaded again for him to get help for her baby but her pleas went on deaf ears. Having had enough, Officer Bond opened the car door and tried to pull her from the car. But being as she was strapped into her seatbelt this proved difficult. He continued to pull her by her hair and shoulders to get her out. The whole time she is screaming "my baby", witnesses would later say. In an attempt to get away and to her son, Shantae puts the car in gear and pulls into traffic. Officer Bond who is out of the way of the moving car at this point pulls his service weapon and aims into the moving car. He shoots from

93

point blank range hitting both driver and back passenger killing them both.

Over the past few months Marcus had been preparing himself for this very moment, and now it was here. He drove past Bond's house and he could see that he was in the living room. Marcus could not help but think about his father and how he died. He did not want to end up like that, at least not until his mission was complete. The chill of the late October night air was just what Marcus needed right now, because his nerves had him sweating like he had just run a marathon. He had been over the details of how he was going to do it a million times, but now that it was time, he kept thinking of all the things that could go wrong. Marcus took one last deep breath and rang the doorbell. Marcus could see Bond walking to the door.

"Yeah who is it?" Bond's deep voice said.

"It's Jeff Tatum, your new neighbor."

Marcus had done his research and he knew that Jeff Tatum had indeed moved in only two days ago. Aaron Bond opened the door.

"What can I do for you-"

He saw something that did not quite register. Number one from everything he heard Jeff Tatum was white! And second why the hell was he holding a gun? But before his brain could send a warning signal to the rest of his body, Marcus fired a single shot that entered his left eye and sent a parabellum bullet barreling through his brain. Marcus looked down at the bloody but still breathing Aaron Bond he said,

"Justice for Shantae Bridges."And fired two more shots into his face and head.

The last year and a half was not easy for Marcus. He quit the police force, telling everyone that he was too damaged by what happened to continue. Some thought he was doing the right thing for quitting, others thought he was a coward. Marcus quit the force but not before doing some research.

He compiled a list of all of the police shootings from all over the country. He referenced that list with the Social Security database. And he came up with a list of names of people who had escaped justice for far too long. The day that he was finished with his research was his last day on the force. As he was leaving the station for the last time with his belongings, he ran into a detective named Mendez. He and Mendez were friendly and had hung out a few times after work.

"Marcus, I heard you put in your papers."

"Yeah I think it's time." Marcus said simply.

"I'm sorry to hear that I think that you could have been one hell of a cop. Your piece of shit of a partner on the other hand, "Mendez said speaking of the now deceased Holmes.

"Why were you so hard on him, if you don't mind me asking?" Marcus wanted to know.

"I will gladly tell you!" Mendez said

"A few years before you joined up Holmes and his partner were out on patrol. Holmes, hot for some action wanted to go to the projects and rattle some cages. His partner Phillips was a vet and he wanted nothing to do with it. So, Holmes sees some black dudes minding their own business and he decides to bust their balls. As it turned out those dudes were a couple of badass gangbangers who had just finished serving some serious time for a lot of evil shit! And of course, they're strapped and ready to kill before they are returned to prison for possession of a weapon. So, it goes without saying that the shit hit the fan!"

Marcus thought he knew where this story was headed.

"He bolted?"

"Exactly!" Mendez said. "But that's not the good part. After running from a gunfight and leaving his partner with his ass blowing in the wind. He runs into a house for "cover" he would say, and he accidentally discharges his weapon, and kills a woman who lived in the house!"

Marcus jaw drops.

"What happened, how the hell did he get away with that?" Marcus asked.

Mendez looked away and wouldn't make eye contact.

"You know that we take care of our own and with a little creative thinking we made it look like the bangers did the deed. "Mendez said before saying, "I just thought you should know who you were riding with."

Marcus moved back home to Virginia, and quietly went to work putting his plan into action. He went to his father's old bunker and decided he was going to do some renovations. This was now going to be his home. Even though he still owned the family home, he just could not bring himself to live there. But he would keep it and use it as his mailing address.

As much as he wanted to withdraw from the world and focus on his mission he knew that he could not do that. He had to blend in. So, he opened *Tanner Industries*. He made a lot of money from defense contracting but the real reason he opened Tanner Industries was cover for his activities. He could buy explosives and guns and would all appear normal.

As word of the murder spread, he quickly realized his mistake. The media was saying all of the wrong things about why Bond was dead. It was speculation that it was a love triangle gone wrong. And Marcus's personal favorite that it was a group Muslim extremist who targeted Bond for termination because of Shantae being a Muslim. He and Bond were the only ones who knew why he was dead, and he wanted the whole world to know. But even with no one knowing what he did, it didn't matter. He knew! He knew that he was making a difference. Marcus knew that he was standing tall for all of the faceless people who could not stand up for themselves. When he thought about the look on Bond's face before he took his life, it was enough to give him goosebumps.

He was so excited that he decided right then and there that he was not going to waste anymore time. It was time to get back to work.

Being that Marcus could work when he wanted to, that meant that he could spend time doing other things such as plotting out his latest mission.

At the present moment he was in a motel room in sunny San Diego, California. He was looking intently at a video of the incident that had brought him to California. The video was of a police shooting of a man named Larry Owens Jr. The saddest part of the Larry Owens Jr. story is that he was shot on his wedding night. Larry had just left his wedding reception and was on his way to the airport to go away for his honeymoon. He and his new bride were in a rented white Ford Taurus. Larry pulled over to the store to buy a pack of cigarettes. What Larry didn't know at the time is that the police had gotten a description of a light-colored sedan in the area that had been involved in a robbery and a shooting. From what authorities said the shooting and the robbery were drug related. When Larry went inside the store, he was being followed by unmarked police cars. As Larry walked out of the store, he made eye contact with his wife as she sat on the passenger side of the car, they both smiled. At that moment one of the unmarked police cars pulled up and grabbed her out of the car and had her face down on the ground before she knew what was happening. Larry ran to his wife's aid but was tackled by officers from another car. Somehow Larry was able to break free and that was when he realized they were police, and he quickly put his hands in the air. By this time all the police had their guns out and were pointing them at Larry. Everyone was screaming for Larry not to move. A loud noise is heard. Some say it was a car backfiring, but no one was ever sure. Whatever it was it caused one cop to discharge his weapon. The next thing you know Larry was cut in half by a hail of bullets. One officer was so caught up in the killing frenzy believing he had been shot at, he actually unloaded his weapon and popped in another clip and shot Larry again as he lay dying. The four cops involved were cleared of any wrongdoing by the department and the prosecutor declined to attempt to bring the case before a grand jury to seek an indictment.

There was never any justice for Larry Owens…until now.

Marcus had been able to track the four cops down with no problem. They were not hiding, quite the opposite actually. They seemed to be going on with life as usual. Tonight they were at a bowling alley, playing in a charity game. The four cops played on the same bowling team. Marcus had actually come to watch them play, they were really good.

Marcus had trailed them off and on for the last week and he knew that tonight they would all meet up for bowling practice. The bowling alley they practiced at was almost deserted on this Wednesday evening. They practiced for almost two hours before they all came out and stood by their parked cars.

"Hey Ray, what's with the tickets to the Padres game I asked you about."

"I have to go and pick them up, you're good to go." Raymond Santiago replied

"What is it babe?" Melvin Pierce said as he answered his cell phone."I am on my way now; we just got finished just now."All of the men laughed

"You are so pussy whipped!" Laughed Pete Harper.

As Pete laughed he saw something or someone out of the corner of his eye that almost made him choke.

"Gun, GUN, GUN!" He yelled as he sought cover but it was almost too late.

Marcus was dressed in all black, including a black mask. Santiago was able to draw his weapon before Marcus got a bead on him with the AR15 but he died with his gun in his hand when Marcus shot him twice high in the chest. This gave the other officers a chance to seek cover behind parked cars. They all returned fire in the direction where Marcus was standing only seconds before, now only air was there. But he would soon make his presence known as the AR15 came roaring to life from only a few feet away. Another of the officers was shot in the throat and drowned in his own blood. And just as fast as he attacked, he was gone. Peter Harper was looking around for the shooter trying to make it to safety. Marcus popped up three cars away from him, and Pete took off running. Marcus shot him in his back as he ran.

Pete rolled under the car after losing the use of his legs. Pete expected the shooter to come and stand over him and he looked all around for him, when all he had to do was look to the left,

"Hey, you." Marcus said and Pete looked under the car as Marcus was laying on the ground with the AR15 pointed under the car right at him. He squeezed the trigger and sent Pete to the afterlife. What Marcus or the cops did not know is that a few cars down a kid by the name of Kevin Mays was on his lunch break smoking a joint when all hell broke loose. He had the presence of mind to pull out his phone and stream the gunfight live on social media. At the same time Marcus was chasing down the last surviving cop who made it to the doors of the bowling alley. The cop ran out of bullets not too long after the shooting started. He threw his useless gun to the ground and said,

"Mister I got kids! Don't do this, please! I'm a cop, you don't want to kill a cop!"

Marcus stood silent and pointed his gun at the cop and said "Justice for Larry Owens Jr."

"Aww fuck!"


**ONE HOUR LATER**

The crime scene was bedlam. It was pure chaos. The news smelled blood and they were out in force

."Can you tell us anything?"

"Do you know what happened?"

"Sometimes reporters ask the dumbest questions!" Detective Tony Rizzo said to a young police officer.

"Tell me something useful Rizzo." Barked the Chief of Police Franklin Parker.

"What we do know is that somebody or some people took out four of our best and brightest."Rizzo said looking at one of the bodies under the light of the crime scene techs."This has got to be some kind of coincidence right? No one in his right mind would walk in here ready to duke it out with four cops and think that he was going to live to talk about it…right?" Asked a stunned Chief Parker. The implications of what had just taken place started to simmer in his mind. "This can't be happening…"

"Chief take a look at this," the tech pointed to a single sheet of paper on the ground .It read 'Justice for Larry Owens Jr.'

"Oh My Lord Jesus!"


**MEANWHILE**

*"Breaking news just in. It is being reported that four San Diego police officers were gunned down just a short while ago. And it was all streamed live on social media!"* Even Marcus was stunned by this development!

*"The wild shoot took place at the Right Up My Alley bowling alley just a short while ago. Hold on I have some breaking news coming*

102

in." The anchor said and held his finger to his ear while he listened to the new information. *"It is being reported that the four slain officers were the very same officers that were involved in the shooting of Larry Owens Jr. Owens was shot only hours after his wedding by four cops in a case of mistaken identity. The officers' names were Peter Harper, Raymond Santiago, Melvin Pierce and John Old man. All of these officers were cleared of any wrongdoing in the shooting of Owens."*

Marcus turned the channel and it was pretty much the same story until he got to CNN.

*"In a turn of events a man by the name of Kevin Mays live streamed the five-minute-long gunfight on social media."*

Marcus got online and logged into his Facebook account. He could not believe what he was seeing! Better yet he could not believe what he was reading! The comments were amazing to say the least. So many people had reacted to what happened, and they let their opinions be heard! Marcus spent the next few hours just reading the comments and gauging people's reaction of what he was doing. Not to say that all people agreed with him, because that was clearly not the case. But the people that he intended to reach had definitely heard him loud and clear! It was while he was reading the comments and messages that he came up with the idea of responding to them. He could not do it on his own page, but he could make up a page dedicated to the cause that he was fighting. One of Marcus's hobbies was that he was an internet junkie. In no time at all he had everything he needed in place. To put it simply he made it impossible for anyone who might try to track his messages back to him. He made up an account on all social media platforms and began posting his messages.

By the time Marcus was back home in Virginia the internet was going insane!

No one believed it was really him, so he decided to go on Facebook live. After setting up his camera, he put on an executioner's type of mask and began.

"To all poor and oppressed people everywhere. I have begun to wage war on our oppressor! This country has been desensitized by the wholesale slaughter of poor oppressed people. The police kill us and go unpunished. We kill us and act as if it is something to be glorified! But today I say no more! I am one man willing to lay down my life for what I know is right. I have no fear of my enemy, but my enemy should fear me. Because, I am living my life as an example of how we should react to oppression and tyranny. I will fight until I take my last breath, and if you watch me and pay attention, I will teach you to fight too! Death to our oppressors!"

When Marcus walked off screen all that was left on the screen was a banner that hung on the wall that said poor oppressed people everywhere.

"Marrow, Connolly can you two step into my office for a minute please?" Requested Special Agent in Charge Donald Treadwell.

"Have a seat." After the two agents were seated he said, "I take it you have been watching the news lately?"

Both agents nodded and Treadwell continued.

"We have a real situation on our hands with the thing in San Diego. The media has taken to calling him the POPE. It is an acronym for Poor Oppressed People Everywhere. This guy has the nerve to have a Twitter account!" Treadwell said, shaking his head. "This nutcase has already killed five police officers and if we don't stop him he will kill a lot more."

Agent Marrow raised her hand to interrupt. "He killed four in San Diego, not five."

"I was just getting to that." Treadwell said and slid a copy of a file across the desk. "The fifth cop or actually the first cop was a man by the name of Aaron Bond. He was Cincinnati PD, he got into a bit of trouble-"

"Killing an unarmed woman named Shantae Bridges and her baby." Marrow interrupted again.

It dawned on Marrow where all of this was leading.

"You mean to tell me this POPE guy is killing cops who for lack of a better word got away with murder?"

"That is exactly what I am telling you. And you two will be in charge of catching this son of a bitch."

The POPE was everywhere! Marcus could not believe what he was witnessing. Anywhere he went the POPE was on everybody's mind. He was a godsend to the media who gave his story around the clock coverage. Also, he didn't have to worry about the world not knowing what really happened to Aaron Bond because it was growing speculation that he was behind that murder as well. But what absolutely blew his mind was the way that the youth were responding. They were at the forefront of the movement from the very beginning. They had taken to starting their own Chapters of the POPE in cities around the country. Marcus had to admit that he was a little proud of that fact. Take for example, a city like Chicago where 500 poor kids are murdered every year by another poor kid. Now a big percentage of those poor kids were at least listening to him and focusing that hopelessness and anger somewhere other than on themselves. But Marcus had to ask himself was this the right direction? Where exactly was he leading people to? Was he trying to get a whole country full of angry youths to start running around and killing cops? Because if he was not careful then that is exactly where all of this would lead to. But one step at a time, he at least had them focused on something other than killing each other and that was no small feat.

### PRESENT DAY FBI HEADQUARTERS

"I do not see how allowing these guys to take over the investigation will help us catch this guy."Agent Marrow pleaded to S.A.C Treadwell.

"Marrow my hands are tied on this. This thing is growing into something that none of us have ever seen before. And with the copycat killers pledging themselves to this guy, let's just say that it

is making some very important people lose sleep at night."
Treadwell said and led Marrow to a conference room where
officials from the Department of Homeland Security were waiting.

"Donald it has been too long." Replied John Ross Deputy Director
of Homeland Security. "How is Emily and the kids?"

"There great, John Jr. has just been accepted to WestPoint."Ross
said with pride."But enough about all of that let's get to business
shall we?" Ross said.

"First off I am not trying to step on any toes here. I think that given
the circumstances that the FBI is doing all that they can to catch
this madman."

"I feel a 'but' coming" Agent Marrow interjected.

"But I think that with all of the resources that Homeland has at its
disposal it is better equipped to handle something like this. As you
can see this thing has started to grow and mutate into something
too large to contain. And that brings it squarely into my
jurisdiction."

Marrow wanted to argue but deep down she knew that he was
right.

"The most important thing is that we catch him and put him down.
Hard! And maybe that will serve as a message to all of the
wannabes out there that look up to this scumbag."

When Deputy Ross finished talking you could hear a pin drop.

"I will be leaving Ms. Alicia Bailey here to work hand and hand with you. She speaks for me in all matters as it relates to this case. Gentleman, Ladies, if you will excuse me, I am expected at the Whitehouse to brief the President directly on this matter."

With that Ross and his team were out the door, leaving Treadwell, Marrow and Baisley. Treadwell could feel the tension and said,

"I will leave you two ladies to it." And quickly made an exit.

The two women stood there looking each other over.

"So, what's your game plan?" Marrow asked.

"I was thinking that the best way to catch a narcissistic asshole like this was to wait for him to go live and trace him some way."

Marrow just smiled, because she had been thinking the same thing.

"The only question is how? We have some of the best techies in the world and they couldn't figure out how to pin down a location or who really sent it."Marrow stated.

Now it was Baisley's turn to smile."I think I may know a guy. But I must warn you, this is how should I say it...Totally fucking illegal"

"As long as it gets this guy, who gives a fuck! Besides, he is not going to court, he is going to a funeral...His."

## A SHORT TIME LATER

Baisley and Marrow pulled into a housing project in Southwest Washington D.C.

"Where the hell are you taking me?"

Marrow asked looking around at the tenants of said housing project. The residents in return eyed the two of them suspiciously.

"Trust me I am about to make your day Agent Marrow."

Marrow rolled her eyes before saying,

"We will see about that."

They entered the courtyard that led to the front door of one of the many identical housing units. Baisley knocked on the door which was quickly opened by a little girl who couldn't have been more than five years old.

"Hey there Bianca, is you Uncle Ronnie home?"

The little girl responded by opening the door wider to invite them inside. Bianca smiled up at Baisley and said,

"I remember you. You used to bring me and Ronnie presents after he had his accident."

Agent Baisley returned the little girl's smile and said, "You are so smart, you remembered me!"The girl nodded and ran off to go get her uncle.

"Accident?"Marrow inquired.

"The accident she is talking about is her uncle Ronnie getting shot in the back at close range with a 44.Bulldog."

Marrow grimaced when she heard this and said,

"There is no way he could walk after that-" She cut off her sentence as the man she assumed was Ronnie rolled into the kitchen.

"Agent Baisley what do I owe for pleasure?" Ronnie said in his deep baritone voice that did not match the diminutive man in the wheelchair.

"I really hate to intrude like this, but I really need your help. I don't have anyone else that I can turn to."

Ronnie nodded his head one time and said, "Follow me."

He led them to a bedroom that had been for all intents and purposes turned into a computer lab.

"I see you're still up to your old tricks."

Ronnie only shrugged at this and said "Hey someone has to pay the bills around here."

As if dismissing what he said Baisley waved her hand and replied

"I could care less how much money you steal from those fat cat corporations. I just really need your help. I know that you have heard about the POPE that has been in the news lately."

"How could I miss something like that? The kids in this neighborhood love him!"

"I was wondering if it would be possible to set a trace, and the next time he goes live, you could lead me to him?"

Ronnie went quiet for a while as he seemed to think this over.

"Agent Baisley as much as I respect you and what you done for me and my family. I can't help with this one."

"Can't or won't?"Baisley shot back.

"If this was like the time I helped with the dude that was selling kiddie porn on the dark web. Or the dirt bag that was hiding the Mobs money in offshore accounts, but this is different."

Baisley was quiet while she waited for him to explain further. When he did, she was blown away.

"You don't get it do you? This man is a HERO where I'm from! But you two could not relate to that because you have no idea what it is to be black in this country! This is the only man that I have seen fight the pigs back and live to tell his story! This is HISTORY right here! And I will be damned if I go down in history as the man who sold him out! Now can y'all please leave my house?"

"Once they were back in the car", Marrow said,

"What the hell just happened in there? Do you really think that people think that he is a hero?"

Baisley looked off into the distance like she was thinking of something.

"I don't know but I have an idea. It hit me as Ronnie was talking about not wanting to be the one who sold him out. But I am willing to bet that someone else would."

## TWO HOURS LATER

"We have no new leads on the killer of seven police officers known as the POPE. And that is the reason I am here to beg the public for help. Somebody is watching this right now and they know exactly who this killer is. Well I am here to offer a twenty-million-dollar reward for the capture or killing of the man known as the POPE.I know that in some communities in this country this killer is some sort of hero. A man who in his own twisted logic is bent on getting justice. But what he is after is revenge not justice. He is a cold-blooded murderer. So, to that person who is watching, and you know who this killer is, I want you to know that you are not a sellout. YOU would be the HERO! Thank you."

Marrow left the podium and Connolly and Baisley were waiting.

"So what do you think?" Connolly inquired.

"I think someone is about to be twenty-million-dollars richer."

---

Marcus had found his man. He stood a good distance away and just watched him interact with the people who had shown up for today's event. Marcus thought to himself that Shawn Butler looked a lot bigger on TV. Marcus did his homework on Shawn. He had a degree in civil law, and he owned a small practice. Shawn was very vocal in the movement to protect America's citizens from those that were supposed to protect and serve. But what sealed the deal for Marcus was Shawn's reaction to the copycat shooting in Newark, New Jersey. In an impassioned speech he said.

"I am here today to tell you that right is right, and wrong is wrong! The killing of unarmed citizens is wrong! But on the other hand, the murder of police officers in the line of their duty is wrong! There is no room for that in this movement. So if you are only here so that you can kill innocent cops who are only trying to do their job, and a very hard job I might add, you are in the wrong place!"

It was then that Marcus knew what he had to do.

"It's now or never." Marcus thought to himself as he made his way closer to Shawn. As he approached he started to second guess himself. The next thing he knew he was standing right by the man he had come to see.

"Ah, Mr. Butler? I am proud of the work that you are doing out here."Marcus said flashing a smile and extending his hand.

"Thank you and your name is?" Shawn asked, shaking his hand.

"Marcus, Marcus Tanner. I have been following your movement closely and I would love to know more about it."It was something in the way that Shawn looked at him that made him uneasy.

"Let's cut to the chase. Who sent you?"Shawn said, shooting daggers at Marcus.

"I think there has been some kind of misunderstanding. I have not been sent by anyone. Like I said I have been following you and the movement in the news and I wanted to know more, but I see that I may have been mistaken. I think that I will go now."And with that Marcus began to walk away.

"Wait, Mr. Tanner, please forgive me. I have been under a great deal of stress as of lately. I have been harassed from every branch of law enforcement, from the local police to Interpol. So please forgive me if I am a little suspicious of a man who appears out of nowhere and everything about him screams COP."Shawn said laughing, breaking the tension.

Marcus laughed as well and replied, "In full disclosure, I did in fact use to be a member of the LAPD."Shawn stopped laughing and said,

"Really? Tell me more."

"There isn't much left to tell really. I did it for a while, and it got to a point where it was the same thing day in and day out. Poor people going to jail and being killed. I got burned out really fast."

"And that was it? That's all it took for you to walk away?"

Shawn replied and waited for Marcus's reply. Marcus was quiet for a second while he thought about how much to say to this man that he did not even know. In the end he decided to be truthful.

"I was involved in the shooting of an unarmed teenager, named Tyrone Dunn."

Shawn was familiar with the case and responded.

"You're the partner presume?" Marcus was surprised and a little impressed that he was so well informed in the topic of police shootings."But from everything that was reported in the media it seemed to be a righteous shooting. "Marcus did not answer." Unless you're telling me that all of the facts were not made public?"

Marcus still did not answer but he made eye contact.

"Motherfucker! Did you and your partner, may he burn in hell, kill an innocent kid and make it look like he killed a cop?"

This was not the way that Marcus envisioned this going but he decided to go with it.

"Is there somewhere we can talk, in private I mean?" Shawn led Marcus to a trailer that had been set up as office space for the rally that was being held today. Once they were seated, Marcus began by saying,

"Like I said, I have been watching you and your organization very closely. I know for instance that you are a lawyer by trade. "Shawn nodded and agreed.

"Yeah that's right."

Marcus nodded at this and took a dollar out of his wallet and slid it across the table to Shawn.

"This is a retainer."

Shawn raised an eyebrow.

115

"I usually charge a little more than this but, go on."

"Being that you are now my lawyer, I believe that anything I say to you is protected under client/lawyer privilege, right?"

Shawn nodded "It's a little bit more complicated than that but go head, you have my attention." This was the moment of truth.

"My partner shot and killed Tyrone Dunn in cold blood. I was in my squad car running Dunn's name for any outstanding warrants when I see the kid take off his backpack. The next thing I know is that my partner is pulling his gun and …."

Marcus was quiet for a few seconds while he relived the events of that horrible night all over again.

"My partner killed that kid right in front of me. And he wanted me to help him cover it up. He goes into the trunk of our squad car and he pulls out this little gun, puts it into the kid's hand and says we can make it look like the kid pulled it out."A single tear slid down Marcus's cheek." I look down at that poor boy and I can't help but to see my Mikey. "Shawn was so riveted to his seat that he did not dare interrupt him." Mikey was my little brother and he was killed by a man that was a lot like my partner. I looked down at that boy and I bent down to tell him that I was sorry and that I wished I could have saved him. But when I bent down it was like something took over my body. It was like I was outside of my body looking at myself. The next thing I knew…the gun was in my hand. I pointed it at my partner, and I squeezed the trigger."

116

This was the last thing that Shawn expected to hear. But if he thought Marcus was wrong, he was silent.

"But that is not what I came to tell you. The truth is that from that night on I knew what I had to do. My partner was the first cop to die at my hand but he was not the last. I am the reason that all of you are here today. I am the POPE."

For the first time in Shawn Butler's thirty-four years he was speechless.

"Why did you come here? Why tell me all of this?" He managed to say.

Marcus was asking himself the same question but deep down he knew the answer.

"You understand the cause and what is at stake with all of this. You understand what a moment like this means in the history of our people and this country as a whole. You know without strong leadership that the movement, you and I see growing all across the country, that if it is not guided right it will burn the entire nation to the ground. My actions started all of this, but I can't damn sure be out there front and center leading, now can I?" Marcus asked Shawn but he did not respond, but he knew he made his point.

"But you can lead! Shit you already doing it!"

Shawn got up and walked to the small window in the trailer and looked out at all of the people. The young and the old. People who all came to support the man who was standing right next to him asking for his help.

"What do you want me to do?"Shawn asked knowing that this decision would change his life forever.

"I need you to help me not totally fuck this thing up!"


**FORTY -FIVE MINUTES LATER**

Shawn stood on the stage that had been erected for the speakers at the rally and looked out over the crowd. A feeling had overcome Shawn after speaking with Marcus and laying the foundation for something that was needed and really, long overdue. The host introduced Shawn and for the next few moments it was as if time had stopped.

"Brothers and sisters, I come to you today with some really important news. Or should I say a message. Today I was contacted by the man we are all united here today to support. I was contacted by a man claiming to be the POPE!"

The gasp in the audience was loud.

"I had the opportunity to engage the man I believe to be the man we are all in support of in a conversation. A conversation that changed my life. It was a conversation that brought me to the ultimate goal"

The audience was silent in an almost trancelike state as Shawn spoke.

"First and foremost, this is not about killing law enforcement. They have a very necessary function in our society. Those that have escaped justice shall receive justice! From this day forward brothers and sisters who are poor and oppressed we are UNITED! Forgive and forget whatever petty difference that you have had in the past. Whatever they may have been, it was because of your Poor Oppressed state! We put all of our focus now on our Oppressors! When we throw off the chains of our oppressors they will declare war and try to put us back in our predetermined places!"

Shawn looked the crowd over with an intense stare before he continued

"But I am here to tell you they have already begun to wage war against you! Oppressed people around the world have been slaughtered and herded like sheep for far too long and today, we say, NO MORE!" The crowd erupted in unison!

## CHAPTER 5

"*H*ow is it going so far?" Marrow asked Connolly, as she handed him a much-needed cup of coffee.

"You don't want to know. You would think that if the government offered twenty million bucks up for this guy that people would be in lines to serve him up. But we got exactly nothing, zip, nada!"

Marrow sat down with her coffee and began to read the psychological profile of the un-sub, hoping to find something that she may have missed.

"Oh, here comes your new bf." Connolly said as Baisley walked into the office.

"Awwwww that's so sweet, you're jealous!" Replied Marrow with a smile.

"Guess who just spent the last hour getting her butt chewed off by the Commander in Chief?" Baisley said, clearly pissed.

"Sit down and tell us what happened."

Marrow replied offering a chair to Baisley who took it and put her fingers to her temple and began to massage them.

"The short and less profane version is that he is livid! He wants results and he wants them yesterday! He is threatening to declare

Marshal law and suspend the Constitution! But the really scary part is that he said he would lock up all of the POPE followers and charge them as enemy combatants."

Marrow and Connolly's faces must have shown the shock that they felt because Baisley said "That is the same way I looked. And the crazy part is that he is serious."

Everyone there knew that if the President carried out those threats no good would come of it. The only thing that would happen is that the country would end up tearing itself apart.

"There is one piece of good news that came from my briefing with the President. He said whatever it takes to get to get this guy, do it. Then he said I will repeat WHATEVER! Any collateral damage he said is on him and he would take care of it."

Everyone sat there in silence for a moment while they thought of the ramifications of what they just heard. Marrow was the first to speak.

"We have a serial killer who only kills a small portion of the population. How many people could it really be on his to do list?"

"Thirty-eight." Connolly quickly shot back.

"That's right thirty-eight. So, what that means is that those thirty-eight poor bastards need to have eyes on them 24 hours a day! I want round the clock surveillance on each and every one of them starting right now, in the hope that our friend pays them a visit."

Baisley and Connolly nodded liking the sound of the idea.

"If he comes within a mile radius of any of them, we will be waiting with so much firepower he won't know what hit him!"

At that moment an agent named Jeffery came running into the office at full speed.

"You have got to see this!"

The agent nearly shouted, before turning the television on.

*"It would seem that the individual known as the POPE has made contact with this man."* An image of Shawn Butler appeared on the screen. *"At a POPE rally in a show of solidarity with the most wanted man on the FBI Most Wanted list. A crowd of an estimated five thousand people showed up and they were not disappointed. The organizer of the event Shawn Butler told a stunned crowd that he had been contacted by the POPE! He also relayed a message to the crowd and to the world. He called for peace among the poor and oppressed people around the world and to focus fighting the oppressor."*

"We need everybody focused on finding everything we can about this Butler guy ASAP!"

After that everyone in the office was running around at a frantic pace.

"He is a lawyer that specializes in Civil Rights law. He also has a PHD in African studies. He graduated from Yale and then attended Harvard law. He has been practicing law for the past ten years. Butler was always vocal in his opinions about police brutality but never anything that would be considered as radical as this POPE guy."

Marrow took in all of the information that was flowing her way.

"Anybody thinks this Butler guy could be the shooter?" Baisley and Connolly both stopped what they were doing and looked at Marrow. Connolly was the first to speak.

"We can't rule that out, but my gut is telling me no."

"As much as I would love for it to be this easy, I don't think it is him either." Agent Marrow's phone began to ring and she answered it, listened to what was said as she grabbed her jacket and raced out of the office. "We have eyes on Butler!" She said as she ran.

By the time they arrived at the area where agents had Butler under surveillance, Butler was surrounded by a wall of POPE followers who were acting as protection from a crowd of reporters who wanted to talk to him. Marrow, Baisley, and Connolly made their way through the crowd and came face to face with Butler.

"Mr. Butler, FBI, may we have a moment of your time?" Marrow said flashing a smile as well as her credentials.

---

Meanwhile, Marcus was only a few miles away and he thought to himself, "This could not be good. "as he watched live footage of Shawn being led away in handcuffs. Having followers was not something that Marcus planned for. But, now that he had them, he needed help in guiding them in the right direction. Shawn had given him that help. The goal is to unite poor and oppressed people around the world. No matter your race or religion. Shawn knew that as soon as he let it be known that he was in contact with the POPE he would become a marked man. So now it was time for his part of the plan that they had put together. Marcus donned his mask and stood before the camera.

"Today I have set in place the foundation of what this movement stands for. Today you have heard from the man I designated as the spokesman for the POPE movement. He is the embodiment of the movement. He is the only one that I allow to speak on my behalf. It is him and only him who is to be contacted on any and all matters related to the movement. I will release my manifesto to the world. It will explain my goal of making oppression a thing of the past, so that future generations may experience true freedom. I will not lie to anyone who can hear my voice right now. War is inevitable. We must first identify our oppressors. They have had a millennium to perfect their craft. They have even taught us to oppress ourselves. It is a misconception that I have chosen to wage war against police who unjustly kill its citizens. I have declared war on the system that allows them to go unpunished. The police have unwittingly become co-conspirators of the government and big business corporations, to exploit and oppress the masses. The police convey the message from their masters that it is ok to kill us because we are looked at as less than. They have been fooled into thinking white is better than black, black is better than brown. Rich is better than middle class, middle class is better than poor. While they watch us kill and fight each other over that ideology. The police are unaware of most of this, but they still know the difference between right and wrong. Not one of those ever accused of killing an unarmed civilian has ever apologized for their actions. So, what that tells me is that in their mind, what they are doing they think is right......

And so is what I am doing!"


### FBI HEADQUARTERS

"Mr. Butler do you know that I could lock you up right now and you will never see the light of day again?"

Shawn Butler sat with his hands folded on the table in front of him, staring at Marrow and Baisley.

"I was contacted by a man who I do not know. I talked with him and shared the conversation with those at the rally. I do not see where I have broken any laws."

"Well according to the Patriot Act you are assisting a terrorist group." Baisley said.

"Oh, so you have labeled us a terrorist group now? Because as far as I know it is one man and one man who has acted on behalf of the POPE.

"Bullshit you have people lined up all across the country to ambush cops who are out there only trying to do their job!"

"If anyone has acted out of some misguided belief than that is very unfortunate. I was given the guidelines and the doctrine that we now operate under. I was asked to deliver a message to the people and that is what I have done. Now I have a message for you. If you are not careful with how you proceed, you will bring war to every city and state in this great country of ours."

"What is that some kind of threat?" Marrow wanted to know but deep down in her heart she knew that he was right.

"Agent may I have a word with you?" Interrupted S.A.C Treadwell, who had been on the other side of the double glass.

"This was just received by the Washington Post."

He handed her what looked like an essay of some kind.

"It's his manifesto. I have sent copies to the Behavioral Science Center to get their take on it, and to see what they can add to the equation."

Marrow looked at the paper in her hand and could not wait to read it and try and get a feel for the man that she was after.

"Oh and before I forget."Treadwell said as he began to walk away." Take a look out the window."

Marrow looked at him, not sure of what to make of the request. She did as he asked and when she saw what he was talking about her jaw dropped. As far as she could see it was filled with people. More specifically POPE supporters. Some held signs others wore t-shirts. But they all had one thing in common, that they all looked mad as hell!

"Once you finish your interview with Butler, cut him loose, but keep an eye on him."

A short time later Shawn was released, and the crowd went wild when they saw him. The crowd that filled the area was enough to almost bring Shawn to tears. Someone handed him a bullhorn and he addressed the anxious crowd.

"I thank each and every one of you for letting your voices be heard today! It is because of you that I am free and here to share this moment with you. Today is only the beginning of the governments' harassment of any and everyone associated with us and what we stand for. But we will not be deterred! We will not sit by while oppression and injustice goes on any longer in this great country of ours. To the brother we have taken to calling the POPE. Our POPE. I want to thank you for your bravery and courage. You have brought all of us together for a common cause and we will not let you down!"

**ONE WEEK LATER**

As Marcus went over his plans for his latest mission, he was not the only one making plans.

"I want all eyes to open people. I don't have to remind anyone that we have a vicious killer out there on the loose trying to kill the guy in that house." Agent Marrow said over her walkie talkie. Right now, there were agents staked out and watching every officer who had been involved in a police shooting.

"I have to say this Templeton guy is a brave son of a bitch. "Baisley said as she looked out of the van that was used for a stakeout.

"I mean to be willing to be used as bait while a murderer stalks you like an animal is kind of hot."

Marrow turned her head and looked at Baisley.

"I will admit that he is tall, dark and handsome but do I have to remind you that the 'brave son of a bitch' you're referring to was charged with unloading his service weapon into a van full of illegal immigrants?"

"I know, I know." Baisley whined. "But he is still...kinda, hot."

Marrow just shook her head.

Meanwhile, Marcus was watching the house and in his gut something just did not feel right. He thought that it was something with his escape route, but after checking that and seeing everything was in place, he could not shake the feeling. As he was listening on his radio to the sound of local law enforcement as well as the federal, he did not hear a peep. Marcus decided to make another swing past the house and if it was clear, then he would move in.

It was on this last drive past the house that he caught her attention.

~~~~

"I could swear that the car has been through this block at least twice already." Marrow said to no one in particular. Before anyone could respond, Marrow said, "Pull over that car!"

The gold Toyota Camry had only one passenger that she could see.

~~~~

Marcus felt the trap before he, actually, saw anything. And he reacted right before they pounced. Marcus hit the gas and the car leapt forward right as two unmarked cars attempted to box him in. He swerved and avoided them.

"It's him! It's him! All units move in now!" Marrow shouted over the radio.

It was as at that moment that the whole world lit up and the dark residential block was now brighter than Times Square! Police swarmed from all directions. As Marcus reached the corner of the block, he saw that they were attempting to set up a roadblock. He cut hard to the right and jumped onto the curb and shot past them. Marrow saw this and went ballistic.

"I want that car stopped now! I don't care what you have to do to do it, but stop that son of a bitch!"

There was little to no traffic out and Marcus made the most of it. He swung his car into the opposite lane and turned down a side street that held a surprise for the police. Seeing where Marcus was headed, a dozen police poured into the small side block in pursuit. It was exactly what Marcus wanted. In Marcus's lap was a cell phone and when he looked into his rearview and saw that the police were in position he hit Send. The explosion caught everyone off guard. The car that was parked by the curb went up in a ball of flames and sent fiery shrapnel tearing through the police cars like a hot knife through butter.

"What in the fuck was that?" Marrow screamed as she saw what happened. "Back up!" Marrow said as she witnessed what lay ahead of her. She did not want to get caught up in the pile up that the roadside bomb had caused.

Marcus saw that his trick had worked but he knew that it would only be temporary. He knew that he had to get out of the area as fast as possible. Local law enforcement had now joined the chase and was now speeding through the street hot on Marcus's tail. He continued his escape, while looking at the flashing lights on his phone. It was a GPS type of device with flashing lights all along the route he was traveling. When Marcus saw that he passed all of the flashing lights he hit SEND.As they chased him down a long stretch of city street, roadside bombs went off, one after the other. Cars exploded with the IEDs that Marcus had placed in them for an occasion such as this.

"It looks like a war zone out here!" Baisley said in awe.

It was with a very heavy heart that Marrow said, "Break off pursuit. I repeat break off pursuit!"

With all of the explosives going off, Marrow could not take the chance that an innocent bystander might get hurt or killed. She watched as the suspect got away.


**HOURS LATER**

"Do you mind telling me what the hell went wrong tonight? Because I was roused out of bed an hour ago by none other than the President of the United States himself! And let me tell you he was not pleased." Treadwell said as a way of a greeting.

Agents Marrow, Baisley and Connolly knew this was coming, but they still did not know what to say.

"Sir I have never seen anything like this before. We are dealing with someone who is clearly on another level. This is not your garden variety psychopath."Marrow replied.

"I understand all of this but you still have not told me what happened."Treadwell stated patiently.

"We had Templeton under surveillance in the event that the subject made a move, and boy did he make a move!" Marrow replied thinking about what had taken place very recently.

"I observed what I thought to be a suspicious looking vehicle making one too many trips down the block, and I ordered the car stopped." Marrow replied as she walked Treadwell through what had taken place. "I think that we need the bomb squad to check any and all cars in the area that are not registered to the residence that they are parked in front of." Baisley added.

Once Treadwell was gone, the three agents had a chance to catch their breath.

"This thing could have gone really bad after what happened tonight." Baisley replied looking around.

"How so?" Marrow shot back wanting to know where Baisley was headed with all of this.

"Look around, what do you see?" But before Marrow could answer, she said "The media! From every news outlet from Fox to Al-Jeezerah! They will have wall to wall coverage on this day and night. And you can bet that he and his band of followers will use this as a way to make him more appealing. Think about it he outsmarted the FBI, Homeland and the local boys, in stunning fashion I may add! It was something out of a Hollywood blockbuster for crying out loud!"

Marrow did not want to admit it, but deep down in her heart she knew that Baisley was right.

"I agree with everything that you said but what do you suggest we do about it?"

Baisley said without hesitation "We catch him or anyone who's helping him carry out his agenda and blow them away."

---

Shawn was not enjoying his new status as the front man for POPE. At the present moment, he was in his apartment looking out the window at the federal agents who made no attempt to hide themselves.

On the television was the latest attempt by authorities to catch Marcus.

Speaking of Marcus, he looked at the prepaid cell phone and dialed the number that Marcus made him memorize.

He picked up on the first ring. "I was waiting for you to call." Was all Marcus said when he picked up?

"What the hell happened out there tonight?"

"They had a trap waiting for me. I felt that something was not right, but I couldn't put my finger on it. Something told me to ride by the house one more time and when I did, they came from everywhere!"

"What the hell were all the explosions about?" Shawn asked.

"My escape plan. In the event that things went sideways, like they did." Marcus said, relieved that he was still a free man.

"Marcus I think that it is time for you to re-think what you have been doing. I believe that you have made your point. You now have the attention of the whole world! We talked about this and now I think that it is time that we move to the next phase of the plan we put together." As hard as it was for Marcus to admit he knew that Shawn was right. He had become a symbol of the fight against oppression and the murder of his people.

"You are right and I cannot argue with your logic, but I have one more thing to do."

Before Shawn could argue his next point, Marcus disconnected the line. Shawn turned his attention to the television and watched as a reporter asked the question

*"What will the POPE do next?"*

"I was asking myself the very same question."

### FBI HEADQUARTERS
### J EDGAR HOOVER BLD.

"Agent Marrow, I have something that might make your day!" Replied Connolly

"I am not in the mood for any of your bullshit today! I am drowning in bogus tips right now. It has been three long months since we got a whiff of our boy's ass!"

"Well I got something that might get us the chance to finally nab that cop killing bastard!"Connolly said waving a stack of papers in the air.

"Here are the lab reports on the explosives that were used in the IEDs the night our suspect got away." He said as he handed over the stack of papers to Marrow.

"It says that the bombs that were used were a specialized device that was popular in Iraq when things were at the worst over there." Marrow continued to read and she said, "So you think our guy was a part of the insurgency?"Connolly shook his head and said, "No, I think he was a part of the surge that was sent in to combat the insurgents! Think about what the profile says, the un-sub was trained in military and law enforcement. So now we know when he was trained and where he served. And if he was able to build one of those IEDs from scratch it is safe to say that was probably his field of expertise."Marrow jumped out of her seat and hugged Connolly and said, "I could kiss you right now!"

"I told you I was going to make your day."Connolly replied with a huge smile on his face.

"We have to access the Pentagon files on those that were deployed in and around Iraq in a time frame that fits the age of our un-sub. And then we cross reference that with the database of every police force across the country and pray we get lucky."

"I don't think that it would be a bad idea to bring Baisley in on this as well. She could cut through a lot of bureaucratic red tape a whole hell of a lot faster than we could." Connolly replied.

"That is not a bad idea at all. I am really impressed you are just full of great ideas today."Marrow said half jokingly.

"I've been eating a lot of kale lately; they say that it's a brain food."

After calling Baisley and bringing her up to speed, they got to work.

A few hours later the trio was in a conference room with stacks of printouts around them.

"The IED in question was in use around 2006 and 2007 so our guy had to be in the thick of it to become familiar with the bomb." Baisley stated and continued saying "They used old mortar shells to make the bombs. That could be another way to track this guy down. Who the hell has access to mortar shells in the USA? It can't be that many people."

"We can use that as something else to cross reference and whittle down the list, because right now there are thousands of people who served at that time, who also went on to be police."Marrow replied as she went through the list of names.

Baisley was looking through the list as well when she came across a name that almost knocked her out of her seat. Marcus Tanner!

"You alright over there, it looks like you just saw a ghost."Connolly said with genuine concern. "No it's just that I saw the name of someone I was really close with at one time on the list of soldiers in Iraq. I had no idea he went into the military he was supposed to join-" "She stopped herself before she could continue.

"Join what?" Connolly asked, wanting to know.

"Oh he was supposed to join the Peace Corps." Baisley said spitting out the first thing that popped into her mind.

She pretended like she was focused on work but the whole time she could not take her mind off of Marcus. *It can't be him.* She thought to herself. She thought about what he told her about his family and what happened to his dad. When she read his file, she saw that he was a part of the Army Corps of Engineers. This has got to be some kind of coincidence. *It can't be him.*

---

Over the past few months Shawn and Marcus worked hand and hand in putting together the foundation of the POPE. They taught their members to be militant minded and the core values of their teaching were to fight all forms of oppression. They both knew that it was a very real possibility that they could both be killed or arrested. So, with that in mind they made contingency plans in the event that something happened to either one or both of them. Their chapters in major cities such as New York, Chicago and Los Angeles were the focal point of the FBI attention but it was the smaller cities such as Detroit, Baltimore and Newark that were the most vicious. For example, there was a shooting of an unarmed man by the name of Hector Alejandro Suarez. An illegal immigrant from Honduras who was shot in cold blood by an officer by the name of Kevin Hanson in Hagerstown, Maryland. The shooting was captured on the officer's body cam. It showed Suarez walking out of a convenience store with a six pack of beer. Officer Hanson was answering a call about a wandering man that was looking suspicious in the area. Hanson approached Suarez with his gun drawn and told Suarez to get on the ground.

Most likely fearing that he would be deported he attempted to flee and ran away from Hanson, who fired his weapon striking Suarez and killing him. Officer Hanson was charged, the case went to the grand jury, and they failed to indict. That night it hit the news that four members of the Baltimore chapter kicked in the front door of Officer Hanson's home. Hanson was sitting in front of the television watching Monday Night Football, when the four masked individuals opened fire, killing him instantly.

Shawn knew that the Constitution allowed that an armed militia be kept at all times to hold the government accountable, and he used that law to legitimize their movement. But he knew that if the killings continued the government's response would be swift and lethal. This became an issue of debate between Marcus and Shawn.

"For those brothers to walk into the cop's house and shoot him down like a dog is no better than what they have been doing to us!" Shawn spat

"And that is exactly the point that we have been trying to make!" Marcus countered. "We have to fight fire with fire! We have to let it be known that this will no longer be tolerated and that if they insist on killing us we will bring the fight to their door steps if need be!"

Shawn knew that what Marcus was saying was right but he felt that if they did not move away from such a violent stance they would never be taken seriously.

"On another note." Shawn began wanting to steer the conversation away from the current debate. "The numbers on our registered members are staggering! At last count we are at well over six million members! I think that we need to think about heading toward the political arena. We have enough members to establish a third political party that could actually win! Or at the very least be a force to be reckoned with."

This intrigued Marcus. "Keep talking, I'm listening." "Imagine the power we would be able to wield over the government. We would be able to influence elections, if not outright win them with those that we choose to run. We have struck a chord with the poor and oppressed in the country and around the world and we have awakened the sleeping giant!"

This all sounded good to Marcus, but he knew there had to be a catch.

"Alright, let's say that I agree with all this, what do we have to do?"

Shawn knew that this would be the hard part.

"We would have to denounce violence."Shawn said simply.

Marcus was quiet while he thought over his response. "I don't think that our position is as solidified as you might think. I believe that if we back down one little bit while we have the oppressors on the ropes, they will turn the tables and end up with their boots on our necks once again." Marcus said passionately. "There will come a time when violence is not necessary, but that time is not right now."

Baisley was finding it hard to sleep tonight. She tossed and turned all night until she finally gave up and got out of bed. Ever since she had come across Marcus's name on that list, she could not stop thinking about him. It was not many things in her life that she regretted but how things ended with Marcus was at the very top of that list. She knew that she had betrayed his trust. If she could go back and make it right, then she would. Knowing that she would never be able to get back to sleep she decided to do a little research. She got on her laptop and ran a check on Marcus's name. It showed that he was LAPD (retired) and that he had served a tour of duty in Iraq in Fallujah. It also said that he had government contracts through Tanner Industries. From what she could tell he was single and never married or had children. She did not know if that was a result of what happened to him as a child or what happened with him and her. Last, but not least she saw that he was still living in the Washington D.C area. It was at that moment that she knew that she had to see him. Every part of her mind told her that this was the man that they were looking for. But her heart told her that this was also the man that she was supposed to spend the rest of her life with.

The next day Baisley took a trip down to Tanner Industries which was located in a nondescript brick building in an industrial park. The front entrance was locked, and Baisley had to ring the buzzer. There was also a camera looking down and soon a voice came over the speaker.

"Yes, may I help you?" Asked the voice politely.

140

"Yes, I would like to speak to Mr. Marcus Tanner."

"What is this in regard to?" The voice replied.

"It is a matter of national security." She shot back and flashed her badge for the cameras.

The door buzzed and Baisley entered the building. She made her way to the receptionist desk and was surprised to see Marcus standing there. He was dressed in slacks and a shirt with no tie. She could tell that he was still in excellent shape.

"Alicia what are you doing here?" Marcus asked with a smile, but also a hint of confusion.

It was almost too hard to believe for Alicia to believe that they were standing here face to face after all of the years that had passed. So many emotions flowed through her that she found it hard to speak.

"Do you mind if we spoke somewhere in private?" She asked.

"Sure, right this way. We can go to my office."

As he led the way to the office he said,

"Can I get you anything to drink coffee, water?"

"Nothing I am fine thank you. You seem to be doing very good for yourself." She replied looking around his office.

"I have been lucky to have stumbled into doing something that I love to do."

"And what is that exactly?"

"I design explosion suppression units for the government." She made him a face to let him know that she had no idea what that meant."Let me explain it to you. Most bombs have a timer or are set off by remote control. If it is on a timer then the unit tricks it into thinking that it has more time than it actually does and keeps resetting the time. If it is by remote, then the unit blocks the signal that tells it to detonate."

"Sounds complicated. Where did you discover this new found passion of yours? The last time we ah…saw each other you were off to join the LAPD."

"I did actually join the force, but I got sidetracked by the war in Iraq. But enough about me, what about you? Last time we spoke you were about to go to Washington to Homeland Security. How did that turn out?"

"It's working out pretty good." She replied and removed her creeds for him to see. "It's actually what brings me here today. I am working the POPE case and I have to be honest with you, you fit the profile to a T!" She said to gauge his reaction and she was disappointed because he had no reaction.

"Is that right?" He said with a smile that revealed his white teeth and the dimple that used to drive her insane. "I am sure that I am not the only person on that list that fits the profile. Let me guess, 25 to 30, black, educated, possibly very well educated. With a military and law enforcement background? Alicia there are thousands of people who fit that profile."

"But your forgetting something Marcus. Something that is not in the profile. What happened to your family is enough to make anybody want justice."

Marcus was quiet for a moment then he spoke.

"I thought about what happened to my family for years. And I let it eat away at me for a long time but I knew that if I was going to have a shot at normal life, then I was going to have to let go. Let go of all of the hurt and pain. And that is what I did, I let go."

The way that he said it made Baisley rethink her assumption about him, and question her own real motivation for coming here. As if he could read her mind he said,

"You didn't have to make up this whole story about me fitting the profile. You could have just said 'Hi Marcus I missed you'." He was smiling again and that dimple was showing and it made her smile in return. After taking a deep breath she said

"Hi Marcus, I missed you."

They agreed to meet for dinner that night and it was just like old times.

For the first time in years Alicia was smiling and seemed to be genuinely happy. They began to see each other and Alicia totally forgot about her suspicions about him. All she knew was that she was back with the man that she loved and nothing and no one would take him away from her again. One night after they made love they lay in each other's arms and talked.

"I have never had the chance to apologize for what I did."

He silenced her by putting his finger on her lips and saying,

"You don't have to."

But she would not be deterred.

"No, I have to. I have lived with this for all of this time. I am truly sorry from the bottom of my heart. You are the best man that I have ever met in my life and I was wrong to hurt you in any way. Even if it was unintentional. I betrayed your trust. I promise you I would rather die before I betrayed you trust again."She looked in his eyes as she said this and he had no doubt that she meant what she said.


## *A FEW MONTHS LATER*

"You think we are in trouble?" Connolly asked.

"I don't know?" Marrow shot back as they sat outside the Director of the FBI office.

"They are going to blame us for screwing up this investigation."Connolly said, clearly scared.

"Will you stop worrying? We did everything to catch the guy."

"I know but it has almost been six months, and no one has heard a peep, Marrow. You know how this works someone has got to be the scapegoat and guess who that is? You and me!"

"Will you shu-"

At that moment the director's receptionist announced, "The Director will see you now."

When they stepped into the office they were surprised to see ASAC Treadwell sitting beside Baisley. Once they were seated the Director got right down to it. I am sure that you are wondering why I brought you here today.

"I am here to tell you as I was just explaining to your boss and Agent Baisley, that all of us are in this together. I cannot stress this enough to you. I had a meeting with the man who currently resides on 1600 Pennsylvania Avenue and he has assured me that capturing or killing this guy is priority number one. He also said that if this guy is not found soon then we will all be looking for a new line of work."When he said this he paused to let the words sink in. "Look I know that you have been busting your humps trying to put this case to bed, but that has not been enough! We need a little bit of luck, and soon because I do not have to remind you that the President can be a little irrational at times. Now go out there and get lucky!"

Ever since Marcus saw Alicia, he knew the clock was ticking. Marcus was not foolish enough to believe that he could go on forever doing what he was doing and not be caught. And if Alicia could figure it out, it was only a matter of time before someone else did the same.

The time that he spent with Alicia was nice, but he was not naive enough to trust her again. Ever since he had been on this mission, he had denied himself the pleasure of a woman's company. So, seeing Alicia was a welcomed distraction. He had succeeded with throwing her off of his trail, but he knew that he had to step up his plan.

Marcus was currently downtown in Richmond, Virginia. He was around the bus station where all of the homeless people congregate. Marcus walked up to a man he saw that was lying inside of a cardboard box and said, "Hey, are you alright?"

"Mister, I am laying in a cardboard box a.k.a. my bedroom, so to answer your question I am not alright."The man managed to say before his body was cracked by a coughing fit.

"Listen I have a deal for you."Marcus began saying before he was cut off.

"Mister I ain't into none of that freaky stuff y'all rich folks seem to be into."

Marcus smiled at this and said "I can assure you I am not rich and not into anything freaky. I just want to help."

The man seemed to think about this for a while before saying, "Help me how?" Before he was once again caught in the throes of a coughing fit.

*Here goes.* Marcus thought.

"I got a big house out in the country and nobody's there but me, and I am barely there. You see I ride by this place every day on my way to work." Marcus lied. "And I see people out here like

146

yourself every day and I got to thinking that all they needed was someone to help them. Well here I am, ready to help."Marcus said with his arms spread wide. The man looked at him suspiciously

"What do I have to do for this to help you talk?"

"You don't have to do anything at all. I just want to help you to get back on your feet."

The man thought about it for a while before saying,

"Alright, we can start out on a trial basis. If I feel like you are not being honest with me I can split and there is nothing that you can do to stop me. Deal?" The man asked and extended his hand to Marcus for a shake.

"Deal."Marcus said, grabbing his hand firmly and shaking it. Marcus helped the man grab all of his belongings and placed them in a shopping cart that was nearby.

"My name is Marcus by the way. What's your name?"

"The name is Julius." He replied in a raspy baritone.

He was about six foot in Marcus estimation but was very thin. When they arrived at Marcus's car Julius started coughing again and looked as if he was about to pass out.

"Julius, you don't look so good." Julius waved him off.

"I am fine. It's just what happens when you live outdoors for as long as I have."

"And how long has that been?"

"Since I came home from the war."

Marcus wondered what war he was talking about, he assumed it was Vietnam based on how old he looked.

"I was in the service myself." Marcus started hoping to draw Julius into conversation, but he did not reply. Then the coughing started again. Marcus gave Julius his handkerchief and he could see when he moved it away from his mouth that it had blood on it.

"New deal." Marcus said. "Before we do anything, we get you checked out by a doctor." Immediately, Julius started waving his hand and dismissing the idea. "They ain't gonna do nothing for me in the emergency room."

"Well we are not going to the emergency room. I will take you to see my private doctor. And I will pay for everything. And I will not take no for an answer."

Julius saw that there was no point in arguing so he conceded. They went to see his physician.

"Well Marcus, I got some test run but they only told me what I already knew and it is not good. He has stage four cancers and it has already spread to his lymph nodes. It is inoperable. There is nothing that can be done for him."

"Well what can I do for him?" Marcus asked with concern.

"The only thing that you can do for him at this point is to make him as comfortable as possible in his last days." The only thing left to say was,

"How long does he have left?"

"The truth of the matter is that he should probably be dead already. But if I had to say, I would say that he will be gone within a month. I'm sorry." The doctor replied before adding, "I will provide him with a prescription for the pain he must be going through but that is all that I can do at this point."

He handed Marcus a copy of the prescription and walked away. Marcus went to the waiting room where Julius was sitting waiting for him.

"I told you they wouldn't do anything." Julius said and smiled revealing a set of black teeth. It was then that Marcus knew that he already knew that he was terminally ill.

"I got one more condition I want to add to our deal." Marcus stated and Julius became weary and replied.

"What now?"

"I want you to get your teeth fixed." Julius just stared at him and burst into laughter.

"Man you are something else! Doctor just told you that I was terminal and you want to spend some more of your hard earned cash fixing up a dead man? Well go ahead then shiiit, I've been wanting the old choppers back for a while now!"

"Good because I know just the place to take you, he has been my dentist for years." As Marcus drove to his new home he thought to himself that his plan was coming together he just hoped that he had enough time.

In the weeks that passed Marcus had to admit that it was kind of nice having someone around that he could talk to.

The only thing that Marcus asked of Julius was that he keeps his dentist appointments, which Marcus took him to.

One day Marcus stopped at his office to get some paperwork with Julius in the car.

"I go to grab some papers from my office, I will be right back."Marcus stated and dashed inside but not before Julius gave him a strange look. When Marcus returned Julius was strangely quiet for the entire ride. He went to the dentist office for his last appointment without as much as a word to Marcus.

Marcus waited for him and when he returned, he was still silent. They drove home and Marcus tried to strike up a conversation and Julius just ignored him. When Marcus got home, he cooked dinner for the two of them. When they sat down to eat their meal Julius said,

"Let me ask you something Marcus."

"Sure anything." Marcus replied, cutting his steak.

"What's your deal? Why am I really here?" Julius said and waited for a response.

"I told you I just want to help you."

"Cut the bullshit, kid. When you first met me, you told me that you drove past where you found me on the way to work every day. But today you took me to where you work and it is all the way on the other side of town, so I know that was a load of horse shit. Now tell me the truth or I am out of here."Marcus thought about lying to him but he saw the look in his eyes told him that he had better not.

"I brought you here to help me fake my death." Marcus said looking him right in his eye.

"How was I gonna help you do that? On second thought don't answer that."

They were quiet for a second before Julius said,

"Maybe I don't want the answer to this, but I have to ask, why would you feel the need to fake your death?"

Marcus didn't skip a beat.

"Because I am the subject of a worldwide manhunt." He said simply.

"You don't seem like the type to be involved in anything crazy. And you certainly don't act like you're on the run. So, there must be something that I am missing here. Why don't you fill me in."Then he leaned back, folded his hands and waited for Marcus to tell his story.

"I am the guy that you have been seeing on television that's wanted for the murders of police officers in several states."

"You mean that POPE fella that has everybody panties in a bunch?" Marcus nodded. "And why if I may ask would you do such a thing?" Marcus paused before continuing, thinking about what he would have to do now that Julius knew his secret. And then as if Julius could read his mind he added.

"It is one of the only benefits of having a terminal disease, you just don't give a fuck about anybody's problems but your own. Now you were saying?"

And with that Marcus told him the entire story starting from the very beginning when he was a boy. When he was done Julius said.

"That is one hell of a story there."

The time had flown by as Marcus talked and he looked at his watch and saw that it was three a.m.

"I think it's time we both get some sleep. Good night Julius, I will see you in the morning." As Marcus was walking away Julius said,

"I only got one question." Marcus stopped, turned to Julius and waited for the question.

"What about the son of a bitch who started all of this? Willy Reeves? Seems like you got some unfinished business there if you ask me."

Marcus smiled and said, "Good night Julius."

As Marcus walked to his bunker, he knew Julius was right. But it was all about timing and William Reeves' time was running out.

The next morning after Marcus finished exercising, he went to the house to make breakfast for him and Julius. After making eggs, bacon and biscuits for the two of them he went to wake Julius up.

"Rise and shine old fella!" And he opened the door to his room. Julius was still asleep "I know you hear me. Come on get up and let's eat our breakfast."

It was then that Marcus touched him and knew. Julius was dead. He was balled up in the fetal position and Marcus walked around the bed and stared into his lifeless eyes. Marcus lost his appetite. He took Julius wrapped in his bed sheets, carried him downstairs and placed him on the floor while he opened the deep freezer. He lifted Julius and placed him inside.

## ONE WEEK LATER

It was a huge rally being held for the new GOP candidate for Governor of the state of Virginia. The speaker who was warming up the crowd for the political hopeful was a star in his own right. His name was Richard Hogan. Hogan was involved with the shooting of an unarmed black man after a traffic stop. The shooting itself was live streamed on social media for the world to see. As can be expected you had a portion of the population in an uproar but you also had a sizable amount that supported him. So much in fact that he was given his own talk show and there was even talk of him running for office himself.

"A vote for the man we are here to see today is a vote against crime! It is a vote against the scum that has been invading our country. It's a vote for good American values! We have criminals terrorizing this country today. A man that is targeting the men and women who wear that uniform proudly and protect and serve us! I wore that uniform and so did the great man that we are here to see today. Before I bring him out let me tell you a story about this man. He was once hunted down by a killer in the home that he shares with his wife and children. A killer who had killed his own wife and child! And what did the system do? It let that animal right back on the streets to kill again! But after being shot at point blank range by that animal he fought him off long enough for back up to arrive. And being the coward that he was he ran! But he did not get far ladies and gentlemen, because he was shot down in the street like the crazed animal that he was! I stood with this man then, and I stand with him now! I would like to introduce the next Governor of the great state of Virginia! William Reeves!"

The crowd erupted as Reeves strode out onto the stage. The crowd was on its feet as they chanted Reeves' name over and over. He stood there soaking it all in, waving at the crowd. It took a few minutes for the crowd to calm itself down before he began talking.

"I just want to say, that is what I call a Virginia welcome!"

And with that the crowd began to cheer again. With Richard Hogan at his side William Reeves stood at the podium and motioned for the crowd to quiet down. When they were silent, he grabbed the microphone to speak, but before he could utter another word his head was haloed in a pink mist. And his body was thrown to the ground. For a fraction of a second Richard Hogan froze, if it was fear or shock, whatever it was, it cost him his life. The shooter fired a second time and hit Hogan on the left side of his chest. It was bedlam at the rally as people ran for their lives. Police swarmed to the stage to tend to the two victims, but it was already too late.

As for the shooter, Marcus was inside a vacant apartment. He had set up his sniper nest against the back wall of the living room. He quickly removed the jumpsuit he had been wearing and took off the latex gloves and placed them in his pocket. He left the rifle where it was as a clue that he wanted them to find later. He calmly walked to the parking lot with a Washington Nationals baseball cap pulled low. He entered his car and drove away from the area. His heart was racing, not because he was scared, but because he had finally got him!


### MEANWHILE

"Shit! You are not going to believe this one!" Connolly said as he raced in the office putting on his FBI windbreaker. "It's looking like he struck again! Two down, white males, both former law enforcement. The first one is Richard Hogan the second is William Reeves!" Marrow could not help but be shocked when she heard the last one.

"The guy that's running for Governor?"

"The same." As they ran to their car Marrow said "I can understand Hogan…but Reeves? I don't get it."But Baisley did. She was quiet as they reached the car and raced to the scene.

"Damn you Marcus!" She said to herself as they swerve through traffic.

"It could be a mistake."Marrow said thinking out loud to calm the rush of adrenaline she was feeling.

"Our guy does not make mistakes."Connolly snapped back and he instantly regretted it.

"But you said they all make mistakes sooner or later. Better sooner than later."

When they arrived on the scene it was chaos. State and local police secured the area as the FBI worked the crime scene.

"Tell me something good." Marrow said to an agent named Brooks who had arrived first.

"It was a political rally with about ten thousand in attendance. The first speaker had just wrapped up and the man of the hour had just taken the stage, when what we figure was a silenced supersonic round was fired because no one heard the shots."Marrow surveyed the area in the distance and said,

"I want agents there, there and there." She said pointing to buildings that looked like good places for a sniper to set up.

Brooks added, "Oh and there is one bit of good news. It would seem that D.C metro had the presence of mind to set up a perimeter, so maybe we got lucky and our shooter is stuck in that huge cluster fuck."

"Agent Baisley? Baisley!" Marrow shouted and she snapped out of the trance that she was in.

"Oh I apologize I was lost in thought." Marrow and Connolly shared a look."A sniper rifle? It's not like our guy." Baisley said, "He likes to get up close and personal. He gets off on seeing them die."

"This is him, I can feel it." Marrow stated calmly. There was a call on the radio.

"Marrow get over to 352 Baldwin, we got something that you need to see."

When the three of them arrived, they were escorted to an empty apartment on the 7th floor.

"Tell me that is not what thinks it is." Marrow said, stunned by the evidence they had just recovered.

"We think that this is the murder weapon. The agent said about the rifle that was left on the floor of the apartment.

"I want some crime scene technicians in here pronto to tag and bag this thing." Marrow said. "You are getting sloppy big boy. Very sloppy indeed." Marrow said to herself as she looked at the newest crime scene. "I want people knocking on everybody's door in this building. I want to know what they saw and when did they see it. Also I want any and all surveillance from around the area so maybe we can get lucky." Marrow said to her troops.

Back at headquarters a few hours later they went over all the details of the case.

"We just got word back from the agent you sent to talk to the family and as would be expected they are devastated. They all say that neither man had any enemies. Well let me correct that, Hogan had a bunch of those from the shooting. Plus, his hard-right view did not endear him to a lot of people as well."Connolly said. "I want us to focus on Reeves right now. What makes him a target for our guy?"

"Maybe it was a cold shot." Baisley added trying her best to steer them away from where she knew this was headed. "I have been reading about snipers and it says that the first shot is the least likely to hit the target, something about the barrel being cold."

Marrow thought about that for a second and said "It could be, but I still want any dirt on Reeves." When she said this Connolly went to his computer and did a search.

"It says that he served 25 years on the force, 12 years of that as the sheriff before retiring and entering politics. He was married to the same woman for 20 years; she was a nurse that treated him when he was involved in a fatal car accident."

This caught Marrow's attention. "Fatal car accident? Who died?" Connolly did some more searching and Baisley thought to herself, "Oh here it comes!"

"The descendants were a five-year-old boy named Michael Tanner and his mother, Andrea Tanner. Oh and get this, "Connolly said and he could feel his blood starting to race "The father who was in the car at the time survived the accident only to be charged with reckless manslaughter. But hold on that is not the good part. It would seem that seven years later Michael Sr. came seeking revenge for the death of his family! He ambushed Reeves at his house early one morning but lucky for Reeves he was wearing a vest and survived. A quick car chase and Michael was surrounded and he opened fired on police and was mortally wounded."

Marrow could not believe what she was hearing. "Tell me somebody in that car survived! Please!" Connolly turned from the computer with the biggest smile she had ever seen on his face.

"You bet your ass there was a survivor! One Marcus Tanner!"

*Oh no!* Baisley thought.

# CHAPTER 6

*A* short time later Marrow assembled the task force to update them on the latest developments.

"We have a person of interest. His name is Marcus Tanner." Marrow said and showed a picture of Marcus from his motor vehicle picture. "He was LAPD but not before serving a tour of duty in Iraq. He was there when fighting was the bloodiest and the weapon of choice was? You guessed it, IED's! Which seems to be a specialty of his and they should be being that he was an expert at bomb disposal. So much of an expert that he invented a bomb suppression unit and sold it to the government. He works as a government contractor right here in the D.C area. Also, he was involved in a police shooting right before he left the force. That case is being revealed as we speak. There was a rifle recovered from the second crime scene in the latest shooting. It is an older model that was popular during the Vietnam War, which is where his father served. The results are not in yet, but we are working under the assumption that he used his old man's weapon to kill the guy he thinks killed his family. As we speak tactical teams are gearing up to take down the suspect who lives in Virginia. I know how hard every man and woman worked in this room to get this guy. We got him! This is him I can feel it! This is for all the cops

this murdering piece of shit killed! Let's go and get this guy!"
Everybody present felt like Marrow was right and that this was
HIM! Even Baisley who slipped inside of the ladies room
unnoticed. She went through her contacts and found what she
was looking for. She heard a familiar voice.

"Hello?"

"Marcus, they know!"

"Alicia? What are you talking about?"

"Cut the shit Marcus! They know and they are on their way to get
you now!"

The line was quiet but she knew he was there because she could
hear him breathing.

"Marcus you there? Marcus?"

"Thank you."

And the line went dead.

Marcus knew this day would come and he was ready. He called
Shawn and then thought better of it and hung up. It would seem
more genuine if when then cops came to question him he was
really distraught. He went to his closet and pulled out a gun but
not just any gun. He got this gun from his connecting Michoski. It
was a Gatling gun that worked by a motion sensor. There was
also a little surprise for them around the perimeter of the property.
This was the part that he was not looking forward to. Marcus went
to the freezer and removed the frozen remains of Julius and

placed him on the floor by the Gatling gun. The last thing to do was turn on a small canister of gas that he had in the room. In the cover of darkness he left the house and made his way through the woods to the bunker. He turned on all of the security monitors and waited. Marcus had it set so that he could control the lights in the house, so that it could appear as if someone was in the house. Time seemed to be at a standstill as he waited and watched, but he did not have to wait long. They approached from the west.

The HRT team was good. He knew they were coming and almost missed them. The team was quiet and made their way to the front door. From the camera he was able to see them place a charge on the door and when it detonated it was followed by a flash bang grenade. When the flash bang grenade went off the HRT team rushed into the house and they were met by a wave of fire. The grenade ignited the gas that filled the air of the room.

*Whoosh!*

As the team scrambled out the house, it was then that Marcus overrode the sensor and started firing. The Gatling gun blazed from inside the house sending death flying in the direction of the HRT team. At the same time one of the surprises Marcus had around his property was detonated, the bomb went off and the police did not know what hit them. The gun continued to spray lead in the direction of the HRT who by this time had retreated to the truck they arrived in and used it as cover. If Marcus had wanted to, he could have killed every last one of them but that was not his intention.

162

"God damn it!" Marrow barked as she watched her worst nightmare unfold.

A short distance away she watched as the HRT was shot to shreds. By this time flames had engulfed the entire first floor of the house. Gunfire continued to come from the house as bombs around the property exploded. It looked like a scene from a war movie. After a while the gunfire subsided, and the explosions stopped.

"I hope that son of a bitch burns!" Connolly said as he watched the fire grow with grim satisfaction.

The FBI had the house surrounded so there was no escape from the inferno.

Baisley wanted to cry and it took everything in her not to give in to the wave of emotion that threatened to overtake her.

Helicopters over the scene carried live images of the gun battle around the world. Shawn was watching CNN when breaking news came with live coverage.

*"It seems that the FBI has been exchanging gunfire with the individual who is believed to be the man known as the POPE. That man's name is Marcus Tanner and he is the man thought to be inside the house that is now on fire after a wild shootout with police. There is no clear indication on how the blaze started. He was wanted for questioning in the murder of multiple police around the country as well as his latest victim gubernatorial candidate William Reeves. It was the murder of Reeves that led authorities*

*here. In news exclusively here on CNN it has been learned that Reeves was involved in a fatal car accident that claimed the lives of the mother and brother of Tanner. His father Michael was ultimately charged with reckless manslaughter but acquitted. Seven years after the tragic accident Michael Tanner stalked Reeves and tracked him down and ambushed him outside his home. Tanner senior was killed in an ensuing shootout with police. To recap..."*

Shawn was stunned as he watched the scene unfold. He told Marcus to stop because he knew that this would be the outcome.

"Damn, Marcus why couldn't you listen!" He screamed and punched the wall in frustration. "What will the movement do now? What will I do now?"

# CHAPTER 7

*T*he powers that be thought the best course of action was no action and to let the fire burn itself out. Bomb squads were called in to the scene to remove all of the remaining bombs that were around the property. Four were found in all. Once the fire was put out investigators entered the house.

"There is no way that he could have survived this." Connolly said as he picked his way through the rubble.

"Hey look at this." Marrow pointed out what looked to be the charred remains of Marcus Tanner. His body was found near the Gatling gun.

"Burn baby, burn!" Connolly sang and it was too much for Baisley

"I have to get out of here." She said and walked away.

Marrow followed her and caught up with her outside.

"You knew him, didn't you?" Marrow asked.

Baisley did not respond, she held her head down. Trying to hold back the flood of tears that she knew would soon come.

"I checked his school record and I checked yours when we first teamed up. I saw that you both went to UNC at the same time." The tears broke free.

"You could say that." Baisley said weakly.

"Oh my God, please tell me you were not involved with this creep!"

"Explain involved?" Baisley said bitterly. "If you mean the love of my life or the one that got away? Then yeah you could say I was involved." Marrow tone softened.

"Why didn't you say anything?" But as soon Marrow said she knew the answer. "You wanted him to get away! You wanted to help that cop killing a piece of hit get away!"

Whatever sympathy Marrow felt for her melted away.

"Did you tip him off?" Marrow asked ready to physically attack Baisley.

Baisley did not answer, she just put her head down in shame. "Oh my fucking God Baisley! That psychopath almost killed more cops because of you! He was waiting for us! He could have killed all of us!"

"I thought he would run, and no one would get hurt. Nobody, not us and not him…"Baisley said and thought of the charred body and lost whatever control she had left. She ran and jumped in her car and sped away. Connolly came out and joined Marrow and said,

"What was all that about?"

"I will explain it to you later; we got a serial killer to identify."

Marcus was still inside the bunker preparing for his departure. He was really going to miss this place; it had really become his home. Once he gathered everything that he planned on taking with him he hit the button and the bunker door opened with a hiss. He scanned the area and saw that there was no one else around. He came out of the bunker and let the door down. Next, he uncovered his bike, climbed on and gunned the engine. It did not take him long to get on the open road. The helmet he was wearing would stop him from being identified so he did not have to worry about that. The next stop was the airport, where his plane was gassed up and waiting for lift off. It was only a matter of time before the plane was traced back to him, this why time was of the essence. He drove right up to the plane and got inside without being seen. The next thing he did was to file his flight plan and ask the tower for permission to take off. Once he had the green light, he shot down the runway. Marcus felt better once he was airborne. He looked at the ground and thought about all the chaos he had left down there to handle. He flew west making his way toward Texas where he had a chartered jet waiting to take him out of the country. He knew that traveling right now, even on a private jet was dangerous, and that's why he had the foresight to purchase a safe house in the area where he could hold up until the heat died down. Marcus thought about what he had been able to accomplish in a short period of time. He also thought what would become of the movement, was there even still going to be a movement without him. Right now, he knew that a lot of brothers and sisters were hurting because they thought he was dead. That hurt him to think about it.

All his life he was taught about leaders that died too soon and the fact he was now added to that list bothered him. But he honestly felt like it was for the good of everyone. He would contact Shawn and he could help him run the movement from behind the scenes.

A few hours later when he finally landed, the first thing he did was take out his burner phone and dialed the only number that was stored. Shawn answered on the first ring.

"Hello?"

"Sorry to worry you brother."Marcus said, not knowing what else to say.

"Worry? I was sick with grief! The whole world thinks you're dead!"

"Good let's keep it that way. Listen I want you to be careful. They will not stop at killing me; they will want to remove whatever remains of the movement as well. I want you to find some strong brothers in the movement and keep them around you at all times to act as your bodyguards."

"We are already one step ahead of you brother. They have been with me for the last week. The FBI grabbed me last night and asked me what I knew about you. I told them the same thing that I have been telling them that you were an anonymous person on the internet. They had no choice but to believe me. I just want you to remain safe."

"You too brother I will be in contact soon." "How does it feel to be a national hero partner?" Connolly said, smiling from ear to ear.

"Once we wrap this bad boy up we have offers from all the networks about sitting down for interviews, we can take our pick! Personally I'm holding out for Oprah."Connolly babbled to Marrow who was occupied reading a report on her desk.

"You did not hear a word I said did you?" Connolly said once he noticed she was not paying him any attention. "I was just going over the preliminary autopsy report."

"What's to go over? They matched his dental records and they could not determine the cause of death because the body was too badly burned."

"I know but it's something that is bothering me. Just can't put my finger on it."

"I know you're just trying to cross your I's and dot your T's."

"I think you said that backwards but continue."

"You know what I meant; the point is we got him! We caught the bastard!! Now I don't know about you but I'm going to bask in the glory of bringing down who the press is saying is "the most dangerous man to ever step foot in this country. So let's celebrate, drinks on me!"

That last comment was enough to get a smile out of Marrow.

"Ok, one drink"

They went to a bar and the entire task force was there to enjoy the major victory that they all got.

"Hey you look…normal." Connolly said when he saw Marrow who had gone home to change into a pair of jeans and a t-shirt with Jimi Hendrix on the front.

"I would like to propose a toast to the greatest collection of crime fighters this side of the Avengers! To us!" Connolly said and threw back his drink.

For the first time in a long time Marrow was able to enjoy herself. She was glad the case was over, but she could not shake the feeling that something was not right. Later on that night after having one too many Marrow made it home and was kicking her shoes off and flopping down on her bed. No sooner did her head hit the pillow than it hit her. The body! Something about the body was not right. She sat upright and whatever intoxication she was feeling drained away. She got back into her car and raced back to the office. She did a search on the internet about bodies that were burned in fires. Marrow worked all night until she found what she was looking for. When Treadwell came into the office she was waiting to show him what she had found.

"Good morning Agent Marrow. I was not aware that we had a casual Friday policy in the office."

"My apology's sir I have been working all night and I think I have something that you need to see."

"Well I hope it will be fast because we have a press conference this morning. Speaking of which, you can't go on like that so I suggest you go home and get changed."

"Sir if you will just listen to what I have to say you may change your mind about this press conference or at the very least change what you say."

"I'm listening."

"Sir something about the condition of the body bothered me for the start. So, I did some research. It says in the report that the house temperatures reached in excess of 2200 degrees. I did some research on what a body is supposed to look like after being exposed to those kinds of temperatures. Our body was bad but not as bad as it should have been."

"So, what are you saying?" Treadwell asked, not liking where this was headed.

"I think the scene was staged and that the body was on ice, which would explain why it was not as damaged as it should have been because it was frozen!"

"So, let me get this right. You think that Tanner killed someone, and that this person had the exact same teeth as he did? Agent Marrow I know that you have put in a lot of hours on this case. I have seen instances where agents become burnt out and start seeing things that are not there."

"But sir," Marrow interjected.

"But nothing. You have done a fine job Marrow. Please don't do anything to mess all of that up. Now if you will excuse me I have a press conference to get ready for."

Marrow knew that what she was saying sounded crazy, hell maybe she was crazy! But something in her gut told her that something was not right. As she studied the reports she came across a file about Tanner's father's service record. It showed that he served as a sniper. That explained why he killed Reeves in the fashion that he did. As she continued reading an idea hit her like a slap in the face. It was one person she knew who probably wanted to believe this guy was still alive more than she did, Alicia Baisley! She was going to help her put this thing to bed rather than she wanted to or not.

With nothing else to do being secluded in the safe house, all Marcus did was watch news coverage of himself. Looking at the people who mourned his death as well as those that celebrated it. His supporters took to the streets. They were angry and hurt over the loss of yet another hero. They made a memorial for him and a very large crowd had gathered together to support each other in these dark times.

Watching the press conference that was held it would seem they brought the story of his death hook line and sinker. But watching the news he saw something else that disturbed him to his core. He was watching the news as they covered the President and he was asked his opinion on the death of the POPE.

"I am proud of the brave men and woman that finally brought down that mad dog killer and gave him the justice he so richly deserved. As of two o'clock this afternoon I sent a directive to the Department of Justice ordering them to make the followers of that killer their highest priority. They pose the biggest threat to national security that I can think of and I want them eradicated" A reporter asked the President what did he mean by those statements and he replied,

"I am authorizing any and all methods to deal with this problem. Today the gloves come off! I want to make an example of this band of misguided fools that made the choice to follow a deranged cop killer. He got what he deserved and soon they will get what they have coming as well! And to the guy at home thinking of becoming the next POPE, wait until you see what happens to his band of disciples. Thank you, that will be all."

Marcus was speechless as the President walked away from the podium.

"Oh my God what have I done?" Marcus thought to himself. Because of him it was entirely possible that thousands if not millions of his followers could die. Marcus did not know what else to do so he called Shawn.

"Hello? I was just about to call you. I take it you have been watching the news?" Shawn began by saying.

"What do you think he will do and what should our response be to that?" Marcus wanted to know.

"I have no idea, but whatever it is we have to resolve this peacefully." Shawn shot back.

"They are talking about eradicating our people! How can that be resolved peacefully? I do not want any of our people hurt, but I cannot stand back and watch them die and not fight back."

"Marcus if we give the order to fight it will be seen as a deceleration of war! How many of our people will die then? How will the masses look at us?"

"I understand what you're saying. And you are right, but I think they already think that they're at war with us! But if you think that you can avoid bloodshed then I am all for it. But if they come in busting heads and shedding the blood of our brothers and sisters then like the president said the gloves are off!"


Marrow knocked on the door of Baisley's apartment. When she answered, she looked as if she had been crying; her eyes were red and puffy. Not feeling the least bit sorry for her Marrow brushed past her and looked around her apartment and said,

"Your apartment looks almost as bad as you do."To her shock Baisley burst into tears.

"Is that what you came here for? To insult me and make me feel worse then I already do? It is bad enough that I almost got agents killed all because I tried to warn Marcus to run but he didn't and now he's dead!"She said as she began to sobbing.

As much as Marrow did not want to she began to feel sorry for her.

"Look, it's not that bad. All of the agents only had minor injuries. Truth be told I don't think your little boyfriend was really trying to inflict much damage. The report on the bombs pulled from his yard said it was only gunpowder. Meaning he only wanted a big bang, he didn't want to hurt anybody or there would have been shrapnel inside the bomb. The way I see it, he was a bomb expert if he wanted us dead, we would all be dead."

"But why would he do that?"

"That is the reason why I am here. I think he did it to put on a big show for the public, the POPE's last stand! So that he could pull the wool over everybody's eyes!"Marrow could see that she still did not understand. "I think that was all a ploy so that your little boyfriend could fake his death!"

She saw the light come in Baisley's eyes when she said the last part.

"That's right sister girl I think he is still alive and that he is laughing at all of us as we speak! Now I need you to help me find him."

While waiting for Baisley to get dressed Marrow said "You told me at the house that he was the love of your life and you let him get away. Well what happened? How did you let him get away?"

"It's a long story but I betrayed his trust by telling my friend about what happened with his father. She in turn told her boyfriend, who was never a fan of Marcus to begin with. He then confronts Marcus with it, and he knew that it had to have come from me and he never spoke to me again."

"But he had to have spoken to you if you knew where to reach him to warn him."

"It was just a hunch at first. I saw his name on a list of people who matched the profile. I could not resist going to look him up for personal reasons."

"Oh I've seen his pictures. I totally understand your personal reasons."Marrow commented.

"Not just that, but to apologize for what happened and the way that we left things and to let him know that I would never betray him again. But once the situation with Reeves occurred it all fell into place. I don't think that I should be involved in this case anymore Marrow. I threw my career in the toilet over my feelings for him. And most importantly I jeopardized my fellow agents."

Marrow knew that she had made a valid point, but she still needed her help.

"Listen no one knows what you told me, not even Connolly. So, if anyone asks you went to school at the same time as he did, but you don't know him. And I need you to get it together because we have to prove once and for all if he is really dead."


**BALTIMORE, MARYLAND**

The SWAT team positioned itself outside of the target location. Based on the Intel that they received, the house was supposed to be filled with weapons and POPE loyalists. An explosive charge was placed on the door and a second later it was detonated.

"Breach!"

The squad leader yelled and the SWAT team poured into the house.

"Hey what the hell?" A man's voice said as he jumped up from the couch where he had been sleeping.

"It's the cops!" Yelled another voice.

From that point on it was pandemonium. It's unclear who shot first but once the first shot was fired the fight was on.

For the first few minutes of the gun battle it was close quarters. The SWAT team was pinned down inside the house with the POPE members, who were convinced the cops were there to kill them all.

"You cop killing bastards!" An angry officer yelled over almost nonstop gunfire.

The house was filled with so much gun smoke that the fire detector was set off. A lull in the shooting gave both sides a chance to tend to their wounded and count the dead. In those first few hectic seconds, everyone involved were fighting for their lives. Once the SWAT team was able to make it back outside that's when the police opened up with everything they had. Over fifty cops fired into the house. The sound of the gunfire was deafening. When it was all said and done two police officers lost their lives and eleven POPE members were killed. There were eyewitness accounts of people being dragged out of the house and they were shot on the front lawn execution style.

## *GEORGETOWN, WASHINGTON D.C*

Shawn had been up the entire night trying to figure out how to stop what he knew now was unstoppable. He also knew that it was only a matter of time before they came for him as well. He and Marcus had put safeguards into place for just this situation. After sending out an email to the POPE Nation he laid down and tried to get some sleep. But he did not sleep for long.

The sound of his door being knocked off of the hinges woke him from his sleep. As soon as he sat up in his bed to see what was going on the bedroom door flew open and a figure in all black was standing over him. Soon he was surrounded, with guns pointed at him. One of the men stepped forward and hit him with the butt of his rifle. After that all he saw was black.

The incident in Baltimore set off a chain of events that would forever change this country. Raids were taking place all over the country in response

To the directive of the President as well as the incident in Baltimore. The police now more than ever wanted to rid the world of any remnants of the POPE. Members of the radical movement were being locked up and killed at an alarming rate. As a result of the killings and arrests a march was held in New York City. To bring the most attention to their concerns the organizers of the march decided to hold the march in Times Square. The tourist attraction that brings in millions of visitors from around the world was besieged by marchers.

"WE will not let you wipe us out!" One of the speakers yelled over his megaphone.

Police with riot gear gathered with the full intention of stopping the march.

"This is the New York City Police! This is an illegal gathering. I order all of you to disperse or you will suffer the consequences."

This was repeated over and over with no one making an attempt to leave the area. The police fired teargas into the crowd and advanced on them with their shields and sticks battering the crowd. The protesters resisted and fought with the police who began to savagely beat anyone in their path. The swarming angry crowd began to hit the police with anything they could get their hands on. The onslaught from the surging crowd was proving to be more than the officers anticipated. There was a fight between three officers and a protester; they were beating him with their sticks and trying to cuff him and place him under arrest. In the heat of battle the officer said to the man, whose name was Joseph Marano, a white male.

"I am going to kill you, cop killing piece of shit!"

Really believing they had every intention of killing him, and that if he let them handcuff and subdue him, he would die. With those

179

thoughts in mind he grabbed for the gun of the officer that was closest to him. The police were so focused on beating him that he did not notice he had grabbed the gun. He stuck the gun under the officer's vest and fired. Two other cops back peddled and pulled their weapons and fired and killed Marano instantly.

But the sounds of the gunfire caused other officers to fire their weapons too. By the time order was restored sixteen protesters lost their lives. Riots began to break out around the country.

Marcus watched all of this in a state of shock.CNN was running nonstops of the events that were taking place across the country. His attention was caught by a Breaking News alert.

*"In the early morning hours federal authorities brought Shawn Butler into custody. The charges have not been announced but it is believed that he will be charged with being a part of a terrorist organization. Shawn Butler is the spokesman for the POPE that is responsible for the deaths of numerous police officers across the country."*

Marcus was numb while listening to him speak, he sat there in a daze. He was brought out of his fog by the voice of the President. Once again, he found himself watching the president express his views on the unrest that was sweeping the nation.

*"The terror movement known as the POPE. Who are responsible for the death of police officers around the country is now considered a radical terror group. Their goal is to destroy the American way of life. I will commit all the power at my disposal, to*

*wiping out this threat. Just as I did their leadership. One of them is on his way to Guantanamo Bay and the other is six feet deep after being burnt to a crisp after having the audacity to go against the United States Government. And all of you out there who are breaking the law by rioting in the streets, you too will be treated like enemy combatants if you do not cease and desist you treasonous activities! This is a fight that you cannot and will not win. I have the law and the power of the U.S military that says that you will lose this fight and you will lose it very badly. For the sake of your loved ones, for the sake of our country go home and stop this now or you will die!"*

Marcus was one of millions of people across the world who watched the president address the nation. Images of the riot and the carnage were broadcast across the airwaves. This was Marcus' worst dream come true. As he sat there, he knew he had to do something but didn't know what. He wished that Shawn was around so that he could talk with him, but he only had himself to rely on right now. And it was at that moment he made his decision

# CHAPTER 8

*B*aisley and Marrow were hard at work digging for clues into

what really happened to Marcus when Baisley glanced at the
television.

"I don't fucking believe this!" A stunned Baisley said as she
watched the news and the breaking news report. Marrow looked
up and she could not believe what she saw.

"Somebody turn that up!" She yelled as she raced closer to the
television.

*"This is a video that is streaming live on social media as we
speak."* The anchor woman said.

*"I have sat here and watched the man elected as the president
attempt to silence you. He attempted to instill fear that you no
longer have. He tried in vain to put the Chain of oppression back
around your neck! But we are not afraid because death is
guaranteed to us all. So, if the only thing you have to fear is death
then there is no reason to be afraid. Speaking of death. The story
that you have heard but about my untimely demise was a
misconception on my behalf. Foolishly I thought that if I went away
they would leave you alone, but the fight would continue. But I see
that the oppressor has become emboldened by what he thought*

*was a victory. They thought that they killed me, and they locked our brother Shawn up. And now they seek to stem the flow that we have created. But it is too late because what started as a drip, turned into a leak which transformed into a flowing river and is now a tidal wave that will sweep across the world and drown any and all forms of oppression!*

*Brothers and sisters across this planet hear my words! Hear my plea for help! We are currently locked in a war with the greatest oppressor this planet has ever known the UNITED STATES OF AMERICA!*

*Those that control this country pray that you will never wake up and realize that you have been misled. Just because you're not black does not mean that you are not oppressed! You are the most oppressed because you are a slave to the government. Your lifestyle makes you dependent and that makes you weak. It makes you look down on those whose oppression is more blatant and you act as if it does not exist! But in order to fight this battle and win, I need you to wake up! I need for those that are oppressed and fighting all across the world to join together. I need the Middle East. I need Africa. I need Middle America to join in the fight of our lives! They thought I was dead, well I have risen from the grave! I have risen from the ashes of that fire as a phoenix to burn the oppressor's empire to the ground! We cannot win if we don't stand together. For all the righteous brothers and sisters who have heard my words rejoice, we will win or we will be in a better place together.*

*And to the oppressors, it is you who should be fearful!"*

The world was at a standstill as Marcus spoke. He had the world's attention and the fight would begin anew.

Marcus' words had indeed resonated around the world. As soon as he was finished talking people in positions of power around the world went into action.

### RIYADH, SAUDI ARABIA

One of those who was inspired by Marcus's words was Prince Ibn Abdul Aizz. The prince was a third cousin to the king and 15th in line for the throne. While he was a very wealthy man indeed, he did not live like most wealthy men did. He lived not in a royal palace but in a very modest home. While most men in his position lived very lavish lifestyles, he was a man of the people. He gave to the poor and his passion was helping in the fight against oppression. Hearing the words of the American had touched him very deeply, for he knew his words to be true. It was his duty to help this man

And that is what he made up his mind to do. After formulating a plan in his mind, he called on his most trusted associate

"Walid I have a very urgent matter for you to carry out for me."

"Anything you wish for, your Highness."

"I want you to use our contacts in American to help with the situation that is brewing in that troubled nation."Prince Aziz said simply.

But it was all that needed to be said.

Walid had been keeping an eye on that very situation as well and had thought of bringing it to the prince's attention.

"I will make arrangements right now."

"Also I want a message sent to their leadership expressing my deepest admiration for his stance, and that if there is anything that I can do to help it will be done."

Later on that night as Marcus was making plans for his return he got a message on social media. The message read urgent and was marked in red. He thought it was some kind of ploy but he answered it anyway. When he clicked on it he saw that it was a message for him it read.

"This message is encrypted so have no worries of outside forces reading this. Your message has been received. The man that I work for wants you to know that he holds you and your movement in the highest regard. Anything that you need will be available to you; all you have to do is ask. As we speak several shipments are in route to every chapter of your organization in your country. If you ever need us just send a message through the link we have provided.

Marcus had no idea where the message came from or who it was from but if they were willing to help then he was grateful. Marcus did not know too many people that were involved in the movement personally, but Shawn had given him some numbers and they had set up passwords to be used with the person on the line. He had waited to initiate contact but now he felt as if the time was right. He dialed the number and waited while the phone rang. Someone answered but said nothing. They waited for him to speak.

"I would like to place an order?" Marcus said the line he was supposed to say.

"Man is the most hostile creature ever created." Was the reply.

Marcus let out a sigh of relief.

"Is it really you?" Said the man who was speaking in a low voice.

"Yeah it's really me." Marcus said back not knowing where to begin.

"I have been waiting for your call since word got out that you were back from the dead." The man replied then added. "That's something you don't get to say every day."Marcus did not know how to respond so he said,

"What did Shawn tell you?"

"He knew that they would come for him. He told me you would reach out to me, but I thought he was speaking figuratively not literally. So, what do you want me to do?" The man asked.

"There is a shipment coming to you. I don't know what it is, but I was told it was something that would help us."

"Well we need it pronto because we have taken heavy casualties. We are being hunted down and killed or arrested. We have wounded who can't be taken to the hospital because they would be locked up or left to bleed to death on a gurney in the hall."

186

Hearing how his people were suffering was painful for Marcus to hear.

"We have tried to make a stand and fight back but they have superior firepower and tactical advantages."

"Listen when the package arrives let me know what it is, and we will plan from there."

Marcus did not plan for all of this and he really did not know how to handle the situation. But if he did not come up with something soon, they were all going to be dead soon. With the rioting and fighting going on across the country the president had decided to send in the National Guard. They were being mobilized and gearing up to ship out. The President had decided to bring this ugly chapter in American history to a close once and for all. Marcus had drifted to sleep when he felt the phone vibrate. He answered,

"Yeah?"

"Sir the package has arrived!" The man on the phone said with excitement."I don't know how you did it but I'm glad you did!"

Marcus was tired of the suspense. "What was in the package?"

"GUNS! I am talking about big guns! And from what I'm hearing they have been sent to every chapter!"

The man went on to tell him that inside the package was an assortment of weaponry. Everything from handguns to rocket launchers.M60 machine guns to hand grenades. Marcus thought about what he was being told and he formulated a plan of action.

"Here's what I want you to do."


## LOS ANGELES, CALIFORNIA

"These are some crazy ass shit homes!" Said a man named Manny.

Creeping along the bushes of a LAPD precinct in the dark of night.

"Man this comes from the POPE himself bro. This is what he wants so this is what we do! It ain't just us this same shit is going down all around the country. It's payback time!" Replied a man named Nesto.

Some of the men present use to be hardcore gangbangers. While others were regular dudes who worked nine to five. They were all shades black, white and brown, united for a common cause.

"You all ready? Let's go!" And with that, the swarm of armed men rushed into the station in Westwood. Before anyone could react 75 armed men poured into the building. A cop at a desk tried to reach for his weapon.

"I would not do that if I were you!" A man hissed as he pointed the assault rifle in the man's face. All the policemen and women were rounded up and placed in the cell block.

"Do it now!" Two men took off and headed for the roof where they unfurled a huge flag. A black and white American flag was hung from the roof of the police station. A POPE flag.

When their mission was accomplished, they raced from the building and sped off. They followed a precise route as they made their escape. The police gave pursuit. The cops attempted to box them in but they had planned for that. As they raced through the city streets with the police hot on their tails the lead driver got on the radio.

"I am coming home for dinner and I brought company with me!"

"Roger that, I will be waiting." The convoy shot passed a block that was lined with apartments as soon as the police entered the block gunman appeared on the rooftops of the buildings. Bullets rained down on the cars. A truck pulled into the intersection of the block as the last getaway car sped by. The driver of the truck jumped into one of the cars. As soon as he was clear a man appeared on the roof holding a rocket launcher. He fired at the truck sending it up into a ball of flames. The cars spit up and disappeared into the dark L.A night.

The convoy of National guards were headed for the Philadelphia headquarters of POPE.

"ETA 20minutes, sir!" Yelled a soldier to his commanding officer.

"It's time to rock and roll, boys and girls! I want everyone cocked and locked! This will be like taking candy from a baby. We will surround the building from all sides. We will then demand that everyone comes out of the building and surrender or else. Once that demand is not met, we have orders to take the building by any means necessary. Is that clear?"

"Yes sir!" Was the response from the troops.

The commanding officer sat back and thought again, "Yep, like taking candy from a baby."

When they reached the destination everyone quickly got into place. When they had the building surrounded, the commanding officer gave the word.

"This is the National Guard! You have exactly five minutes to come out of the building with your hands up. The time begins right...now!"A soldier said over the bullhorn.

"You think they're gonna put up a fight?"Asked a sergeant of his commanding officer.

"I seriously doubt it. They had their fun, now it's serious; once they see us out here, they are going to trip over themselves to come out. And hell, if they don't we'll give some of the boys a little action. What do they get? A couple of AK's and a few small arms? They are no match for Uncle Sam!" Said the cocky officer.

"You now have one minute to come out!" The soldier shouted.

When the count got to ten seconds he began to count over the loudspeaker.

"You have 10,9,8,7,6,5,4,3,2,1,Times up!"No sooner than the words left his mouth

190

Did he hear the whistling sound but even as he saw it he couldn't believe it until someone yelled.

"Incoming!"

As the rocket streaked into the side of the armored personnel carrier. The explosion was deafening. And with that every window on the top floor of the four-story building seemed to spit fire.

Bullets rained down on the national guard's men who were not covered by shelter. The men who had been behind the personnel carrier were the most exposed because their cover was blown to bits.

The National Guard returned fire and the battle was on.

Inside the building the head of the POPE Philadelphia chapter barked orders like a drill sergeant. That's because he was a drill sergeant. When the package arrived, he looked at it like it was a godsend. And it could not have come at a better time. His name was Evan Oliver. He was from rural Pennsylvania and he was a veteran of two tours of duty in Afghanistan.

When he saw what was going on in the country that he loved and shed blood defending, he had no hesitation in joining the POPE.

"Reynolds! Get that M60 up there now!" Oliver yelled. "Debbie, Daniel want you two on the roof. Lob a few of these bad boys there way, Try not to hurt them too bad just get us a little bit of wiggle room because I think it is time to skedaddle!" Handing the twin girls a crate of hand grenades.

"Hey, Oliver over here!" Yelled his communications man Patrick.

"Talk to me Pat." Oliver said looking over his shoulder at the screen of the laptop.

"It seems we have our marching orders." Oliver said with a huge grin on his face.

"It's fucking crazy! But I like it!" Marshall


## THE WHITE HOUSE SITUATION ROOM

"This cannot be true."The President said as he read the latest intelligence report.

"You mean to tell me that they have coordinated strikes all over the country? They attacked the police precincts in over 50 different municipalities. How the hell is that possible?" The president roared. "Also, could someone tell me how in the hell did these people get their hands on military grade weapons?" The president asked his security council. Also present at the meeting was the head of the FBI and the CIA.

"From what we have been able to gather sir, they have been aided by a foreign government." "The Director of the CIA stated.

"What government?" The President wanted to know.

"We are not exactly sure, but in his last message he asked for help from all around the world and it seems like some help has come."

"And You!" The President said pointing a finger at the director of the FBI.

"You get up there and make a big speech about how you caught the guy and killed him and make me look like a jackass because I followed up on those statements!"

"Sir the dental records identified him as Marcus Tanner, the man we were looking for."He said remembering the warning Marrow had given him.

"Well somebody messed up big time! And I will be damned if I get hung out to dry for all of this!" The president said and slammed his fist into the table.

"We have a war raging on the streets of America! This thing is getting way out of hand. We have to find a way to make this thing stop once and for all. Does anyone have any suggestions?"

Marcus knew that he had to make his move and make it now. With the National Guard moving in he knew that if he did not act now a lot more people would die. So, with that thought in mind he streamed his latest message across the internet.

"The time has come to slay the oppressor once and for all! Since they see fit to bring the battle to us, I think it is time we bring the battle to them! You have sent your forces for me and mine, now we are coming for you where you live and feel the safest.

As of right now I issue a directive to any of the POPE members who can hear my voice. You are hereby commanded to head to our nation's capital forthwith! I want all of you in Washington in 72 hours!

Come prepared for the final battle! The clock starts ticking now. For my enemies who have been pursuing me with the hopes of killing and silencing me, for what I stand for, here's your chance because I will be there in the flesh! I will be a man among my people. If we must, we will tear down the White House brick by brick! We will rewrite the Constitution! You have three days so get ready, because we will be!"

People watched Marcus speak and they were in awe! What had started out as one man trying to right a wrong, had turned into something far bigger than he could ever have dreamed of.

As Marcus watched the reaction to his latest post he saw that his members had taken to wearing an American flag but the difference was that it was black and white. They said that it showed the solidarity of the races coming together to fight one enemy. Seeing that warmed his heart, but it also gave him an idea. He wanted everybody who would be in D.C to wear the flag as a mask, that way he would be able to blend in the crowd. As the hours ticked by Marcus made his final preparations. Marcus sent instructions on how he wanted everything to proceed to his followers and he was assured his orders would be carried out. The world was about to see something that they had never seen before after this, things would never be the same again.

## GUANTANAMO BAY, CUBA

From where Shawn sat it was hard to tell if it was night or day. Once he was dragged from his apartment, he was blindfolded and thrown in the back of a van. From there he was taken to another location where they used "advanced interrogation techniques". After that he was sedated and the next thing he knew he woke up here. He was in a single cell with no windows behind a solid steel door. Shawn was wearing an all-white prison jumpsuit with a of pair plastic slippers. Since he had been brought here, he had not seen another soul. His food arrived through a slot in the door. Exactly 15 minutes later someone would arrive to collect the tray and he never uttered a word to Shawn. But all of that was about to change. Shawn was laying on his bunk when the door of his cell slid open. Standing in the hall outside the cell was a man wearing a white shirt, slacks and a pair of aviator sunglasses.

"It is a pleasure to finally meet you Mr. Butler." The man said by way of a greeting

"Who are you?" Shawn said wearily.

"You can call me Mr. Smith."

"Well Mr. Smith or whatever the hell your real name is. You can torture me like your buddies did, but I will not tell you shit!" Shawn said defiantly.

"I admire your commitment to your cause Mr. Butler, but I do not wish to learn any information from you. I wish to share some with you."Mr. Smith paused before continuing."September11thWas over 20 years ago and some of your fellow prisoners have been here ever since, and they have not seen the inside of a courtroom. See they, like you, have been labeled as enemy combatants and not afforded the protections of the Constitution. But you are a lawyer so you already knew that. The point that I am trying to make is that you have been deemed too dangerous to ever set foot out of here ever again. And while you have been here your friend Mr. Tanner has risen from the dead. But it is no matter because plans are being made as we speak to wipe every POPE member off the face of the earth. They wanted justice? Well now justice is about to be served!"

### THE WHITE HOUSE SITUATION ROOM

"There are over one million POPE militants headed in this direction as we speak sir."

"I know that you idiot! I want to know what the hell we are about to do about it?"

"At this point sir I think that is to call in the military." His adviser answered.

"You mean to tell me that you want me to put boots on the ground? On American soil? Are you fucking kidding me? This is the worst thing we could do at this point! It would show the world that this thing is completely out of control! We would look weak to the entire world. No, We have to put this thing down without turning into a goddamn civil war!" The president face reddened as he said the last part.

The Chairman of the Joint Chiefs of Staff who was also in the meeting chimed in.

"With all due respect Mr. President, I don't see any other option."

The president was silent for a moment while he thought of a response. As much as he did not want to give the order, he saw no other alternative.

"Send in the military."He said simply. It was now officially war.

Marcus was in a deep sleep after he gave the orders for the march on Washington. For a short time Marcus was in another world. A world that did not exist anymore. Marcus was standing on the front porch of his house. The house where he grew up. As he looked down the driveway, a single man walked up to him.

It was Tyrone Dunn. Marcus was filled with emotions as he watched the young man walk up to the bottom of the stairs and just stared at Marcus without saying a word.

"I am so sorry for what happened to you that night." Marcus began. "But what I did after you died was even worse. I should have stood up and told the world how you were murdered in cold blood!" Marcus said angrily as a tear rolled down his cheek. "But I was filled with this unexplainable rage that even now I cannot begin to understand. I killed my partner, and in my attempt to cover up what I did…I convinced the world you were a cop killer."Marcus said as the tears flowed freely. "I have been trying to rectify my actions by making sure justice is carried out for people who died just like you did."

Marcus said as he held his head down and when he looked up he saw there was a small army of people standing behind Tyrone. As he looked from face to face, he knew exactly who they were. They were all of the victims. The people who he was trying to win justice for. He made eye contact with Tyrone who looked at Marcus with the traces of a smile on his lips. And he pointed behind Marcus into the house. Looking to where he was pointing Marcus could see his family.

He entered the house and his father was at the kitchen table, while his mom was at the stove cooking. As happy as he was to see them, there was someone he wanted to see even more, Mikey. He moved through the house like a ghost because his parents seemed unaware of his presence. Marcus moved to the backdoor and looked into the backyard where he saw a sight he would always remember. It was his little brother holding up a jar with a butterfly in it.

"See I did it just how you taught me!" Mikey said proudly holding the jar up for his brother to see.

"You sure did." Marcus said, crying.

"I miss you." Mikey replied poking out his bottom lip. "It's lonely here. And I miss you teaching me cool stuff. You were the best big brother ever!"

This brought a smile to Marcus's lips. But before Marcus could reply Mikey said, "I know what you are doing."

This caught Marcus off of guard.

"But I...um" he stammered."

"And I also know why you're doing it." Mikey replied, sounding more mature than his age suggested. "Do you?" Mikey asked.

Marcus woke up from his dream before he could answer, but the question was still on his mind.


## GUANTANAMO BAY, CUBA

"Butler, cuff up!"One of the three officers who stood outside of Shawn's cell said.

Shawn who had just finished his morning exercise said,

"Where am I going?"

"Just do as you're told!" The officer growled. "You will find out when you get there."

Shawn did as he was instructed and stuck his hands through the food port. He was handcuffed before the gate opened. For the first time he was led through the maze of hallways, passing cells that were filled with men from around the world. It still blew Shawn's mind that he was here. He was escorted to a small room where an older balding man white man sat reading a folder that was placed in front of him. When Shawn entered the room the man stood and extended his hand.

"My name is Andrew Fitzsimmons and I will be representing you in this matter."

"And what matter would that be exactly Mr. Fitzsimmons?" Shawn asked, ignoring the hand that was extended to him.

"Mr. Butler you have been charged with some very serious offenses." His lawyer began looking through a stack of papers until he found what he was looking for. "Here we go let me see ah… you have been charged with attempting to overthrow the government, treason facilitating or sponsoring a terrorist organization and last but not least murder!"

To say that Shawn was shocked would be an understatement. "Murder?" Was all he could say?

"Yes Mr. Butler, you have been charged not only with the murders of the police officers with Mr. Tanner but you have also been named as a co-defendant in the how should I say…the uprising that has ravaged the country or some would even say around the world."

The lawyer could see that Shawn was not following.

"I know, I know, beg my pardon. I know that you have been out of the loop in here so to speak." He chuckled before continuing

"Mr. Butler, the country is on the verge of civil war right now! Mr. Tanner has all but assured that by ordering attacks all across the country as well giving a directive for all members to descend upon Washington D.C where he stated and I quote "will tear the white house down brick by brick.""

Shawn was deflated. This was suicide! Marcus and thousands upon thousands would be hurt or killed. Fitzsimmons saw the look on Shawn's face and replied.

"I take it you knew that tales of your friend's death were false." The two men sat in silence for a moment before either man spoke.

"I know that your cause started for a noble purpose. I get that, but Shawn this thing is getting way out of hand! It is the 1960's all over again! Trust me we don't want to go back down that road; I know I lived through it!"Shawn shook his head and laughed.

"You need to tell the police it's not the 1960's! They are the ones killing unarmed people on a weekly basis. You have no idea what people who look like me go through each and every day!"Shawn said heatedly

Fitzsimmons removed his reading glasses and looked at Shawn with tired eyes.

"I know more than you think I do young man. I was pre-law at Kent State in 1970.Do you know what happened on May 4th of that year? I will tell you what happened if you don't know. Four of my classmates died that day. We were protesting the war and the overall treatment of American citizens, black and white, rich or poor. When the Governor ordered in the national guard."Shawn said nothing out of respect for what the man just dropped on him. "So with all due respect I do have some idea of what's happening right now."Shawn was not naïve enough to believe that he could trust this man because he would at least work with him throughout the court proceedings. "The government's indictment also alleges that your organization is in collusion with a foreign government to undermine the Constitution of the United States."

"That is the craziest thing I have ever heard! There isn't a shred of evidence to support such a claim."Shawn said vehemently.

"Once again Mr. Butler I apologize. I forgot that you have been in isolation. In that time several events have taken place to give credence to the government's claims."

Fitzsimmons handed a folder to Shawn describing several incidents such as the one in Philadelphia where POPE militants opened fire on national guardsmen with military grade weapons.

"The CIA is very concerned Shawn. They are of the belief that your organization is being aided by Islamic extremists. This man in particular."

Fitzsimmons said, sliding him a photo.

"Who is he?" Shawn asked, looking at the man.

"Prince Ibn Abdul Aziz. He is 15th in line for the throne in Saudi Arabia. But he is not your average billionaire, it is said that he, in his words, "financed freedom fighters" all around the world."

Shawn studied the man's face and said, "What does he have to do with me?" Sliding the photo back.

"That my friend is the million-dollar question."

## WASHINGTON D.C - FBI HEADQUARTERS

"I need everybody that you can spare in Washington, A.S.A.P!" Marrow barked into the phone. The last 48 hours was pandemonium in the bureau office.

"I got a bad feeling about all of this Marrow." Connolly said once Marrow hangs up the phone.

"I'm listening." She started giving him her full attention.

"This thing has gone haywire! You got this fucker coming back from the grave! And him ordering thousands of people to come to Washington D.C, oh and the best part, he is saying that he is going to be there in the flesh! This has all the makings of a massacre. Once you add the United States military into the mix."

"I don't like any of this either, but this is the hand we were dealt, and we are all in on this one."Marrow replied.

"I see someone has been watching World Series Poker." Before Marrow could respond she saw someone who stopped her in her tracks. Agent Baisley. She looked better than she did the last time Marrow saw her.

"Nice of you to join us." Connolly replied still having no clue of the tension between the two women.

"Can you give us a second?" Marrow asked Connolly, who took the hint and made himself scarce.

"What are you doing?" Marrow hissed.

"I am trying to do my job."

"The last time you did that a lot of agents almost lost their lives. Now the only reason I don't turn you in is because I feel sorry for you."

"I don't want your pity. You don't have any reason to feel sorry for me."

"Oh really? You are so pathetic that you are still carrying a torch for some homicidal maniac who dumped you in college." As much as she hated to admit it the words rang true to Baisley.

"Now if you insist on being here then make yourself useful. Get me as many bodies as you can so that we can stop your boyfriend once and for all."

Marcus had been in the mirror for the last hour trying to get what he was looking for. Marcus had purchased a Hollywood makeup kit and the results were astonishing. When he was done, he was looking at a total stranger in the mirror. Marcus checked his email and saw that he had a message, "green lights all the way". Marcus could not help but smile, his followers did not let him down. Now that everything was in place, he had to think about how he was going to get across the country. With him being the most wanted man in the world, this was no easy task.

When Marcus entered the bedroom a story on CNN caught his attention.

"From all across the country people are pouring into our nation's capital. All in hopes of seeing Marcus Tanner, also known as the POPE." The female news anchor began. "This is a very tense situation. Most if not all of those in attendance are being considered armed and dangerous. And it is for this reason that law enforcement is granting them safe passage to the event in Washington."The story had Marcus full attention as a plan began to take shape in his mind. An older man was now at the podium making a statement. "Although we consider this gathering unlawful and this group criminal, we think that it is in the better good for them to be granted safe passage, to avoid putting more officers needlessly in harm's way. To the members of POPE you are being warned that any overt acts of aggression will be met with deadly force."When he was finished, he was bombarded with questions.

At least Marcus now knew how he was getting to Washington.

A few hours later at a bus station in Jackson, Tennessee, Marcus stood in line as bus after bus was filled to capacity with people headed to Washington with hopes of seeing well...him. He thought as he watched how excited they were. Most of the people wore black shirts with P.O.P.E in white letters. And they also wore the black and white American flag. Also Marcus noticed that most of, if not all of them were armed. He found it ironic that he ordered them there armed and he himself was not. Once he was seated on the bus, he could not help but notice the nervous energy in the air. There were people from all walks of life. Black, white and brown people all heeding the call. Marcus was so caught up in those thoughts that he did not spot the big man in uniform until he was hovering over him. Despite himself he felt like his heart might pound out of his chest.

"Is this seat taken?" The soldier asked.

"No not at all soldier, have a seat." Marcus said, feeling a sense of relief.

Marcus judged his height to be about 6 foot 5 and he had to weigh about 260 pounds and all of it seemed to be muscle.

"My God, what are they feeding you in the army nowadays?" Marcus said in a southern drawl he had been practicing.

"As much as you can eat and all the P.T you can handle to burn it off." The man responded. Marcus knew that P.T meant Physical Training from his days in the army.

"Oh, and I was in the National Guard." The man added

"Was? Well someone needs to tell your tailor then." Marcus said, pointing out the uniform he wore.

"Well I was until very recently. But I saw some things that go against everything that this country supposedly stands for." The man said, becoming serious.

"What happens if you don't mind me asking?" Marcus inquired.

The man seemed to be sizing Marcus up before he went any further, then decided and said, "What the hell? The name is Chet, Chet Graham." Chet said, shaking Marcus's hand.

"Nice to meet you Chet. My name is Aaron, Aaron Moses." Marcus replied giving him the name that was on the fake I.D in his wallet.

"It's a long story, sir." Chet replied.

"Well it's a long trip." Marcus shot back.

"It all started when we got the call to go in and help put down the unrest that was spreading across the country. My best friend Jason was uneasy about getting involved in the situation at all. You see Jason's older brother was killed in a police shooting. We all grew up together and his brother, whose name was James was like a brother to all of us. When he got killed it was something that affected all of us, but mainly Jason. So when the POPE came along, Jason talked about him like he was some kind of superhero or something. And in a way I guess he is or was or, whatever. Anyhow we were sent to Louisiana because there was a POPE faction down there that was raising holy hell! Let me tell you! From the time they thought the POPE was dead they went crazy. So, we got called in and the cops were trying to kill every one of them that they could. And it was not long until my unit got caught up in the madness. On the second night a curfew had been imposed and we were out enforcing it by making sure no one was on the street. We came across a couple of kids. We told them to get off of the street and go home. They told us how their house was burned to the ground because of a black and white POPE flag that was hanging in front of their house. Well that did not go over too well with some of the guys in our division who looked at them as the enemy. Some wanted to beat them while others wanted to kill them, and make it look like they died in the riot. God knows there were so many dead that no one would worry about a few more. When one of the bolder guys named Rooney went to make a move, the only one standing in the way was Jason."Chet took a few breaths to calm himself as the bus rode through the Tennessee night. Marcus said nothing; he would let Chet tell his story in his own time.

"Rooney tells Jason to get out of his way. But Jason refuses. By this time most of our unit has moved on with our patrol. There were only a few of us there. Rooney would not let it go and he made his move. Rooney was bigger and stronger, but Jason was faster. Way faster. For every punch Rooney threw, Jason hit him with three. The fight did not last long. I broke the fight up because Rooney's face was a bloody mess. Jason was talking to the kids when before we knew it, Rooney had his sidearm in his hand. He was pointing the gun at Jason and the kids. Jason reacted by placing himself between Rooney and the kids. Rooney pulled the trigger then I pulled mine."Chet was quiet for a while.

Marcus looked at Chet who had blonde hair and blue eyes but he felt a kinship that was hard to explain.

"I shot Rooney, but not before he killed Jason. After that everything was a blur. Their deaths were considered casualties of the mayhem that had taken hold of the city. We were ordered back to base, but I just couldn't take being there anymore. It was like …"

"Something inside of you changed?"

"Yes exactly. I felt like I had to..."

"Do something that would make a difference?"

"Exactly! And because of how Jason talked about the POPE and how much he wanted to be a part of the movement, I knew what I had to do."

"And what is that exactly?"

Marcus already knew but he needed to hear him say it.

"I want to do what Jason didn't have the chance to do. I want to dedicate my life to the movement." Chet replied looking Marcus right in the eye.

## WASHINGTON D.C

"Sir, as you well know, this may well be the most important case in the bureau's history. And if you don't mind me saying, we screwed up once already and we may not get another shot."Marrow said to herself in the mirror.

She was preparing to brief the Director of the FBI. She was snapped back to reality by a knock at the door of the ladies' room.

"Marrow don't make me come in there and drag you out!"Connolly hissed.

"Can't a lady even take a piss in peace?" Marrow shot back as she exited the bathroom.

"I know that's where you do all of your important thinking. So tell me what did you come up with?" Connolly wanted to know.

"First of all, you know me way too much about me. And secondly if we don't get this guy soon, he is going to lead us into a second civil war!"

They walked into the conference room and they were blown away by who was seated at the head of the table, The President of the United States.

"Mr. President I um…What are you doing here?" Marrow blurted.

"Agent Marrow I presume?" The President asked. As she entered Marrow looked around the table at all the people present at the meeting. Along with the President was the Chairman of the Joint Chiefs, Director of Homeland Security and the Director of the CIA.

The usual suspects the only one who surprised her more than the President was Alicia Baisley!

"Agent Marrow I must say that I am not at all happy with you. Because of you I just fired the Director of the FBI." He paused for a beat to let that juicy bit of information set in before continuing. "You three were in charge of this investigation." He said pointing to Marrow, Baisley and Connolly. "An investigation that was supposed to be closed when that animal died in a shootout and a blazing inferno!" The President roared and slammed a fist into the table. "How is it he was able to fool all of us into thinking he died in that house?"It was then that Marrow spoke up. "Mr. President, we voiced our doubts about Tanner being dead. There was something that felt wrong. And we relayed those feelings to our superiors."

"I was informed of that today, Agent Marrow, which is the only reason that you are still employed, and your old boss is not."Marrow had to admit that she did feel a little bit better knowing that the leader of the free world knew she wasn't a total screw up.

"As you are aware there have been some major developments in the investigation. Things have escalated into something far more serious. It would seem that Tanner and his supporters have been aided by foreign nationals since his return. This group has carried out attacks across the country. But what concerns us most is the latest statement by Tanner." The Joint Chief said ominously.

211

"We are prepared to send in a battalion on a moment's notice to put an end to this thing once and for all!" The President interjected.

"I beg you to show some restraint. I don't think that he will lead his followers into slaughter." She paused to allow them to think and come to the same conclusion she had. "Think about it, he fooled us all! He could be on a beach somewhere sipping mai-tai and laughing at all of us! We thought he was DEAD! The entire world thought he was DEAD!" Marrow said locking eyes with each and every man there. "The only reason he came back was because his followers were being hurt and he felt like they needed him."

"You wait one goddamn minute! You're saying this is my fault?" The President asked testily.

"Not at all sir. I know you did the only thing that you could have done in your position." Marrow stated calmly.

Calming the Commander in Chief down.

"So, what's his play?"Asked Gerald Davies head of the CIA.

"What I believe is that he wants the government to see that he can mobilize the masses into action as a deterrent from further harm coming to his people. The last thing that I think he wants is war. He is smart enough to know that he can't win a war against the United States military." The President was silent as he pondered her words, and then said,

"What's his endgame in all of this?"

"He wants the world to sit up and take notice that the P.O.P.E is here, and they mean business!"

"How sure are you about all of this?" Asked the head of Homeland Security, speaking for the first time.

"I am 100% sure sir" Marrow said with her face stone.

"Well I sure as hell hope so! Because not only your career but the lives of thousands depend on it!" The President stated before adding "Now go ahead and do your job and catch this son of a bitch!"

When they were alone in the hallway Connolly let out a long breath.

"Whoo! You are my hero, you know that, right?" Connolly said half-joking. "Not only did you go toe to toe with the most powerful men in the world, but you looked them in the eye and said 100% sure sir! You rock, you know that, right?"

Marrow just stared at him like he had lost his mind.

"You are starting to worry me." She said.

"No but seriously, thanks for saying "we" voiced our doubt. When in reality it was just you." Connolly replied sincerely.

"I would like to thank you too." Said a voice from behind that saved Marrow from having to deal with Connolly's praise.

It was Baisley.

"*We* owe you for what just happened in there and I owe you a lot more." She replied to Marrow who just stared at her with her poker face.

"Just do your job. Now let's get our shit together, because there is an angry army headed this way as we speak."


## WASHINGTON, D.C

The air in the city was unlike anything Marcus had ever experienced. There were thousands upon thousands of people filling the streets of the capitol. But not all of them were there to show support. The opposition was also there in record numbers.

"This could become a really bad situation."Chet said after taking in the scene that awaited them at the bus station.

"You took the words right out of my mouth."Marcus replied, still in shock by the turn out.

He took in the mixture of those that loved him and those that hated him. As could be expected those that represented the fallen officers were present and very vocal. Also, there are several hate groups. It looked like the Neo Nazis and the KKK were trying to outdo each other. What was of concern to Marcus, it seemed that the law enforcement supporters and the hate groups seemed to have been brought together by their common enemy.

"We have got to find somewhere to crash for the night."Marcus replied.

On the bus ride Marcus convinced Chet that they should stick together. Chet was hesitant until Marcus assured him that he had connections with the POPE higher ups, and he would vouch for him. It was hard getting through the streets because of the sheer amount of people on them. When they finally made it to a hotel, it was clear that it was booked to capacity. People milled about outside of the hotel. When a crowd of anti-protesters arrived and started hurling insults at the POPE supporters.

"You are a disgrace to your race!" One screamed at a red head woman who happened to be white. The opposing crowds went back and forth. When one of the hate group members laid eyes on Chet, he lost it.

"What the hell are you doing over there with them?" He asked incredulously.

"I am where I belong, fighting for what's right!" Chet simply replied.

"Well you should be hung for treason! You are a disgrace to that uniform!"And with that he spit in Chet's face. And then the crowd almost erupted. Almost.

"Wait!"Chet yelled holding his arms out to hold the crowd back behind him.

"You know what? You are absolutely right."Chet said and began taking off his shirt to his uniform. He wiped his face with it and said, "Here you can have it, if you want it!" Chet said and threw the shirt in the man's face. "This is my army now!"

The crowd cheered wildly behind him. Someone threw him a POPE t-shirt and he slid it over his bulging muscles. Marcus had to like the way that he handled what was a tense situation.

"Hey you guys want to come and hang out with us in our room?" Requested a group of young ladies who were eyeing Chet and Marcus, but mostly Chet.

"Sure, lead the way ladies."

A few hours later the party was starting to wind down. The suite that the girls had was crowded with POPE members as well as few people who were just looking for a good time. Marcus and Chet spent most of the night talking about the movement.

"How long have you been involved?" Chet asked.

"Oh I have been around pretty much since the beginning." Marcus said offhandedly.

"I really believe in my heart that with everything going on in this country this is what we need right now." Chet replied.

"How so?" Marcus asked, interested in Chet's assessment.

"Things are really bad right now. You have the government lying and doing whatever they want. The police are out of control. They feel like they can just kill citizens and it seems like they can because they keep getting away with it! And just look out the window, there are Nazis outside right now! Racism is at the highest point I have ever seen it in my lifetime. The last time it was this bad was in the 1960's and I wasn't around for that, but I

216

studied enough in school to know that things were really bad. But you know what? The 60's changed everything! This is why the movement is so important because we are at one of the pivotal moments in history, we can make real change."

Marcus just nodded his head because he could not have said it better himself.

"I want to show you something. I will be right back."Marcus said and walked into the bedroom and got his bag. He opened it and removed his laptop. He logged into his social media account and saw all of the responses he had from the last two days.

"Whets all of this?" Chet asked looking over his shoulder.

"This is the movement!"

He clicked on live stream after live stream from all over the area.

"These are my eyes and ears." Marcus said looking at Chet.

He could see understanding come into Chet's eyes.

"No way!" Chet said not believing what his mind was telling him.

Marcus began removing the nose and other parts of his disguise. When it was all removed, Chet stood there with his mouth open.

"Chester Graham, I am Marcus Tanner. Please meet you."

"Listen up people, listen up!" Connolly yelled, getting the attention of the dozens of people gathered.

"It's Showtime! This could be our only shot at getting this psycho!"

"Making sure Tanner ends up dead or in a cell is priority number one!"Marrow said to the crowd. "If you see anyone that remotely resembles Tanner, call in!"

All of the agents present were dressed to blend in as best they could. Marrow was dressed in black pants, boots and a black POPE sweatshirt. She completed the look with a black and white flag around her neck.

"Let's get out there and get lucky!" Marrow said and all of the agents began to move out.

"You know you look pre-" Connolly began saying.

"If you finish that statement you will lose a body part."Marrow hissed.

Once they were out on the street Marrow said, "My God, they are everywhere!"She replied looking at the ocean of humanity that flooded the streets of the nation's capital. When they got within walking distance Marrow got out of the unmarked sedan and said to Connolly.

"I need you back at the command center. Listen out for any calls about any sightings sent in the coordinates A.S.A.P."

"Marrow be careful out there." Connolly said seriously.

She told him that she would, and she set out across the mall. It amazed Marrow how many people showed up to show their support or disdain. Police delegates from all fifty states showed up in the hopes of finding Tanner themselves. She noticed how the

218

police watched the POPE supporters with blind hatred. Somehow, some way they had to find Tanner in this massive body of people.

"Hey where are you from?" Replied a young guy with red hair and scraggly red beard.

"Beat it loser!" Marrow said instinctively.

"Whoa my bad."

The man said holding his hands up defensively.

"Just trying to be friendly, to one of my POPE Sisters that's all." The man replied and turned to leave.

Marrow remembered she was undercover and slid into her role. "

I am so sorry I thought you were some other loser."Marrow said with her biggest smile.

"No harm. My name is Larry; I'm from Hartford, Connecticut."

"Hi Larry, nice to meet you my name is Jennifer and I am from Boulder, Colorado." Marrow replied, extending her hand.

Larry took her hand and said, "I didn't know we had a Colorado chapter."Marrow quickly responded.

"You don't or we don't, but I have been watching things unfold on TV like everyone, so when he called, I came."

Larry seemed to accept this.

"Well we are set up in delegations of what chapter you're from but being that you're not from any chapter you might as well come with me. Marrow wanted to refuse but thought better of it.

"Alright cool."

She said and followed Larry. At least now she had someone to be her tour guide through this mad house.

Meanwhile, "I don't know about this Marcus." Chet protested.

"Trust me, just do everything I told you and you will be fine."Marcus assured him.

"I said I want to be a part of the movement, but I didn't mean this!" Chet said, starting to panic.

"Chet, I know that you can handle this. Our paths did not cross by chance. This was something that was meant to be!" Marcus said looking him in the eye. "Now get your shit together soldier, we have work to do!"

At that moment there was a knock at the door. It opened and a young man who had been partying with them stuck his head in the door.

"You guys better get going it's almost time to see the PO- .You...man you're the POPE!"The dreadlocked young man said excitedly.

"What's your name kid?" Marcus replied, walking toward the man.

"Gary sir, Gary Williams." The man said the star struck.

"Alright Gary, do you know how to work a camera?" Gary nodded that he did.

"Alright then let's record a message to our brothers and sisters out there."Marcus said and walked in front of the camera.

When Gary gave the word, he began.

"Welcome to Washington, brothers and sisters. Our nation's capital. As many of you know I was born and raised not far from here. For me this is where the movement began. It was here that I lost every one that mattered to me. My mother, my father and my brother. A little boy named Mikey. They were murdered by a cold-blooded killer named William Reeves. Mr. Reeves is no longer with us, but his evil spirit is alive and well. It is that spirit that causes the killing of unarmed citizens to become the norm. Well if that is the new normal, then so is this! Because if they keep trying to kill us, we will keep fighting! Welcome to the Revolution!"

When he was done Chet and Gary stared at him with awe.

"That was dope!" Gary said snapping out of it. "Can I get a pic for the Gram please?" Gary said referring to Instagram. Marcus thought about it and then said "What the hell. Gary stood to the left while Marcus held the black and white flag with both hands in front of Him. Chet snapped a picture.

"Thank you sir! My Instagram is gonna go crazy!"

"You do know that if you post that picture with me then you will have the entire law enforcement community breathing down your neck?"

Gary smiled and said, "For all the likes I'm gonna get, it will be worth it!"

"It's time we get going."Marcus said to Chet.

They quickly gathered their belongings. When they reached the lobby and were set to go their separate ways. Marcus said,

"There is a very good chance that we will never see each other again, but I want you to remember everything I told you."And with that Marcus was gone.

Chet stood there for a second getting his thoughts together, then went into action executing the plan that Marcus put together.

Marrow was eyeing everyone around her. But a lot of the good it did most of them wore their black and white flags to hide their identities. Which gave her an idea and she did the same and used it as a way to talk into her mic.

"Is everyone doing as terrible as I am?"

"Some people are doing worse; Ramirez got jumped by a couple of anti-protesters. Marrow I got a bad feeling about this." Connolly told her.

"Make that two of us. But if Tanner is really here, then this is the only way we will be able to catch him."

"Welcome to Washington!"

Marrow heard and her attention was drawn to the large Jumbo - Tron screen and the smug face of Marcus Tanner. It was the message that he had recorded earlier.

"Is this live? Because if so, we did all of this for nothing!"Marrow asked.

222

"He could still be somewhere in the city." Connolly replied.

"No, I think that sick fuck is here. I can feel it."

Marcus walked among his followers for the first time. It was a feeling he could not describe with words. He also knew that mixed in with his supporters was the FBI and God knows who else. But just for what he was feeling now getting killed or captured would be worth it. When the message he pre-taped earlier was finished he sent the signal to Chet.

"Let the show begin!"

An image of the word P.O.P.E appeared on the screen. The crowd went crazy.

"Brothers and sisters, you have no idea how it feels to be here with all of you!"Marcus said into the throat mic that he wore. "I thank all of you for helping me to show those that are oppressing and murdering us that those days are no more!" The thunderous reply from those present was deafening. "When I started my mission, I had no idea it would lead to this. This was all of you!" Again, the crowd went wild. "I was just one man. One man who watched his mother and brother die. Not only did they not get justice, but the injustice was when my father was charged! Being charged with murdering his own family and watching the real killer get away was enough to push him to kill. He died attempting to get justice. But not before he raised me into the man that I am today!"Marcus said and the crowd cheered. "I never thanked my dad. But in a way I am thanking him with my actions. Like most kids I rebelled and didn't listen to the things my father taught me when I was young. That rebellion to me to Iraq and then the LAPD." At the mention of the LAPD the crowd began to boo loudly. "I know I hated it too. But I want to tell you about someone I met while I was there. Actually, met is the wrong word, encounter is a better word to describe our meeting. His name was Tyrone Dunn."A huge picture of Tyrone appeared on the screen with his graduation cap and gown on. "This young man changed me forever." Marcus said looking up at the screen with everyone else."One night while out on patrol my partner and I encountered Tyrone. My partner thought he resembled a suspect that had injured a police officer and he wanted to investigate. I should have nixed it because my partner was a coward and a bully. I would later find out that he shot and killed a 78-year-old lady out of fear. He then planted a gun and got away clean. But not so clean that his fellow officers didn't know about it. While they wouldn't tell on him, they would ridicule him without mercy. But back to Tyrone. We stopped him and while I was running his name for warrants, I heard a shot and Tyrone was dead. My partner then asked me to help him. He wanted me to lie and say that Tyrone had a gun. My partner went into the trunk and got a gun out of his gear and put it in Tyrone's hand. I bent down and picked that gun up and blew my partners brains out!" Marcus said and the crowd went wild. He could see that his words enflamed the uniformed police who were present, that was not his intention. "But I did something that I am ashamed of. I lied. I lied to that poor boy and said that he and my partner shot each other." The crowd was silent."But I have been

making amends all across the country one killer cop at a time!"
Marcus roared. "Which is what brings us here today? The system
that we live in allows for the murder of its citizens. So we must
now take our concerns to the front door of the man in charge!"The
crowd cheered and Marcus said "Follow me!" And a large picture
of him appeared on the Jumbo -Tron. It was something that he
filmed early in the day."On to the White House!" The image on the
screen was of Marcus pointing toward the White House. And the
enormous crowd began moving. Inching at first and soon they
were on their way.

# CHAPTER 9

## THE WHITE HOUSE

*T*he President watched the march on Fox News.

"My God, what is this maniac doing?" The President wondered aloud.

'Sir I think it's time we moved you to a safer location." replied the head of his secret service detail.

"I'll be damned if I let this son of a bitch, have me hiding in the basement like a coward." The President yelled. "I am giving you a direct order, that if any one of those bastards so much as set foot on a blade of grass on this property I want them shot on the spot!"

The Secret Service agent whose name was Dempsey responded.

"Be that as it may sir, I still must insist that you relocate to a secure site sir."

The President knew it was protocol, but he still did not like it.

"Not one word of this to the media god damn it! As far as they know I am here in the situation room facing these criminals down! I am going into an election year; the last thing I can afford is to look weak."

The President was whisked away to a bunker that was on the lowermost level of the White House. To ride out whatever was about to happen.

Marrow was swept up in a surging wave of humanity barreling toward the White House.

"Marrow get out of there now!" She could hear Connolly say in her hair.

But she was busy making sure she stayed on her feet and moved with the crowd because being trampled to death was a real possibility when this many people were involved.

"That is not possible right now." She managed to say.

Although she was nowhere near the front of the pack, she could tell they were near the White House now.

"Mr. President I know that you are listening now!"Marrow could hear Marcus say over the speaker.

"I know that we have your attention, as well the rest of the world."Marcus' voice boomed. "I simply want to tell you that according to the Constitution we have the right to bear arms!"And with that everyone held their guns in the air.

"We also have the right of a well-regulated militia being necessary to the security of a free state. And Amendment 14 it goes on to say that a person born in the country has the right not to be deprived of their right to life or liberty without due process! But yet, it's still this very thing going on today and no one does anything to stop it. So, we decided to stop it!"

Marrow looked at the sea of people around her and she saw people that had had enough.

They were determined to get their point across no matter the cost.

"According to Sun Tzu's The Art of War, he speaks of the way. The way is the belief that when the army and the leadership are of the same mind they are unbeatable! Well I am their leader and this is my army!" The crowd cheering was deafening.

The look in the eyes of those around Marrow started to make her feel fearful for the first time. She began to wonder if maybe she underestimated Tanner. Was he really ready to wage war? "You have been proven unwilling to stop violence from happening to those who don't look like you or who are not from the elite of society. But if you are unwilling then we are more than willing to stop it for you!" Marrow looked at the Jumbo-Tron and saw something that she could not believe…Marcus Tanner.

Marcus was at the front of the massive crowd and with the whole world watching he held his phone to his face and Chet beamed the live image onto the big screen. He removed the flag that hid his identity and said to a stunned crowd.

"As you can see, I am really here with you!" The crowd cheered so loud for so long that everything else was drowned out. When Marcus was able to calm the crowd he said, "And to those that wish to oppress us, I have no fear of you. We have no fear of you!

War is something that I do not take lightly but if it is war that you want, then harm any one of my people again! And I swear to you we will tear this country apart and rebuild it from scratch!"The crowd chanted Marcus' name over and over. "My people, our point has been made. I want all of you to go home to your family and your lives. But be vigilant and if the need arises, we will go to war! Now go home!"Marcus said simply and put his flag back over his face and was about to log off. 'One more thing I want to introduce you to Chet Graham." Seconds later Chet appeared on the screen looking nervous. "Chet is my field general and he will coordinate all of the chapters on my behalf. Say hi Chet." Chet still looked nervous but tried to cover it by making his voice deeper.

"How y'all doing?"

"Now everyone go home!" Marcus ordered.

Connolly was about to have a stroke.

"He's here! He's here!" He shouted over the radio.

"Calm down! I know he's here because I am HERE! But that doesn't mean we can find him. And what's the deal with Chet?"

"Graham. It looks like he was in the National Guard. It looks like he was discharged."

It was all Marrow heard before she heard something much more important.

"I'm telling you I partied with the POPE last night! Look I even posted it on my Instagram." She overheard a young man with dreadlocks say to several young women.

"Oh, can I see?" Marrow said getting in on the action.

"Sure see?"He said, holding up the phone so that she could see.

"You have got to come with me, now!" Marrow said, looking Gary in the eyes.

His face frowned and he said, "Go with you where?"

"Chet and Marcus sent me to find you." Marrow shot back quickly.

Gary thought about it before saying, " Lead the way. As they made their way through the dispersing crowd, all hell broke loose.

The anti-protesters began fighting with the POPE members. Those that were there to support the fallen police officers were soon sucked into the melee.

"Go!"Marrow screamed and ran, pulling Gary along with her.

Things were going from bad to worse, when gunfire erupted. That drew the police into the mix and they were out for blood. All around Marrow fighting was going on, but she held onto Gary like life depended on it. It took her awhile to get her bearings and see exactly where she was. She made it into a side street and called in.

"I need all units to, Georgia and Pine ASAP! I repeat Georgia and Pine!"

Gary was shocked. "You're a cop?"

Marrow looked at him and said, "FBI and you are now a witness in the biggest investigation in history." She said ready to subdue Gary if need be.

Marrow looked out to the main street and saw that things were getting worse. It looked to her that instead of breaking up the full-blown riot, the police started using this as an opportunity for some payback.

"I think we had better get out of here." Marrow said when she heard.

"Hey, you two on the ground, now!" Two officers were approaching in riot gear.

"I am a federal ..." Was all she could say before she was silenced with the butt of a gun. Marrow was knocked to the ground. As she tried to stand, she was kicked in the face. She barely hung on to consciousness. She watched helplessly as Gary was put on his knees.

"I'm a..."Marrow said and was again savagely kicked.

"This is how you end this shit once and for all." one of the cops said. And with that he put the barrel of his gun to Gary's head and pulled the trigger.

"No!" Marrow screamed.

"I said shut up bitch!" And once more she was kicked.

"C'mon Oscar, you do her, I did the last two!"the officer said to his partner, looking around.

The young cop raised his weapon eager to prove himself. He placed the gun to Marrow's head but before he could pull the trigger, a blur came from nowhere. He grabbed the cop and pointed his gun away from Marrow. In the struggle the cop squeezed the trigger, and bullets leaped out of the gun. Out of the corner of his eye the stranger could see the other officer pointing his weapon. He grabbed the officer's arm and pointed the gun at his partner and the last four bullets out of the clip slammed into him, but not before he returned fire. He could feel the cop slump in his arms lifelessly. And he let him fall. The man who was hit once by the return fire looked down at Marrow. Who looked at him with disbelief in her eyes.

"It can't be!" And then everything went black.

Chaos ruled the day. The violence was on an epic scale. Marcus was surrounded by this, not to mention the two dead cops, and one dead POPE member. And he had yet another that was in bad shape, but she was alive thanks to Marcus. He knew that he had to get out of the area and soon. Marcus felt terrible that he could not have acted in time to save Gary's life. He scooped up Marrow in his arms and carried her into the street. Police and ambulances were everywhere, attending to the wounded. Marcus saw an EMT crew patching up a few injured people and noticed the engine was running. No one paid attention. Marcus laid Marrow in the back and closed the door. Before anyone had noticed he was driving away. He put on the EMT jacket that was in the driver's seat. Marcus removed his flag and turned on the sirens and drove as fast as he could. It took him awhile to get out of the area, but once he did there was not a cop in sight because they were all back at the riot.

He pulled into a deserted underground garage and went in the back to check on his passenger. She was still unconscious. Looking at her something, struck him as being familiar. Once he started attending to her wounds, he saw the earpiece. A quick search turned up a transmitter as well as her identification.

"FBI." He said reading her badge. It then dawned on him where he knew her from. Marrow awoke and had no idea where she was. She tried to sit up but got dizzy immediately.

"Take it easy I think you have a concussion." Marcus replied.

She looked at Marcus who was shirtless tending to a bullet wound in his shoulder. Seeing the hole took her back to when she was about to be killed.

"I guess I owe you." Marrow said and Marcus ignored her. "Where are we?" Marrow replied looking around at the vacant home.

"Why so you can call your friends to come and save you?"

Marcus said holding up the transmitter and the earpiece.

"Ok so you know who I am. I know who you are, so we are even. But my question to you is why are you still here playing nurse and not on your way out of the country?" Marrow wanted to know.

"I was but I saw you and someone I knew in trouble and well you know the rest."

"Alright since you are in the mood to answer questions, who the hell do you think you are? Who gives you the right over life and death?"

Marcus looked at her as if she had lost her mind.

"Excuse me? Do I really have to explain that to you after what almost happened to you?" Marrow knew he had a point but she could not let him off the hook that easy.

"You set the stage for all of this. You took it upon yourself to take the lives of…"

"Of who? People who got away with murder!" Marcus said emotionally. "They killed people for no other reason then, they could! And the system backed them up so that it could happen again and again!"

"Alright but where does it end? People died today Tanner! I almost died today! The streets of our nation's capital are soaked in blood right now. Now I ask you again where does it end?" Marcus thought about his answer for a moment before he answered.

"It ends when they stop killing us." Marcus said simply.

He then went about bandaging his shoulder. Seeing that Marcus got hurt while saving her life made Marrow feel guilty.

"Thank you." She said looking away."You saved my life and as much as I hate to admit it, I owe you." Marrow said sincerely.

Marcus said nothing to this, but he did acknowledge her with a nod of the head.

"I'm still going to take you down when I get the cobwebs out of my head." She said, laying back down.

"I wouldn't have it any other way." Marcus replied.

"Oh, and before I pass out, I know about you and Baisley." Marrow said with her eyes closed. Marcus was shocked by this, but he knew it was only a matter of time before someone made the connection.

"She was innocent in all of this." Marcus said to Marrow.

When she did not answer he looked at her.

She was sound asleep.

The President kept his promise and he did send in the army. But they were there to help restore order. Connolly was on the scene as well.

"I want eyes on every dead or injured person." Connolly said hoping against hope that Marrow was alright.

"Have you heard anything yet?" Baisley said walking toward him.

"Nothing. No sign of her. It's like she just vanished off the face of the earth." Connolly said distraught.

"Connolly I think I got something!" A young agent said excitedly.

"I have been going through all of the video footage in the area. Well there was an alley not far from where Marrow called in her location. They found two dead D.C cops and a kid named Gary Williams who was shot in the head. We got lucky and got a video. I'm warning you it's a bit graphic."He said and played the video.

It showed Marrow and Gary enter the alley. Soon after they were approached by two officers. The cops had their guns out and it looked as if they were being ordered to the ground. The cop hit her with a gun and Connolly flinched. The cop continued to beat Marrow. The other cop shot Gary. When his partner pointed his gun at Marrow Baisley gasped.

"God no!"

When a man rushed into the frame and grabbed the officer before he could shoot Marrow. By the end of the video three men were dead and the unidentified man picked up Marrow and walked away with her.

"Got a report of a missing ambulance, could be connected." Replied the young agent named Sawyer.

"Why would Marrow be with this Gary Williams guy?" Connolly wondered.

"It could have something to do with this right here." Baisley said, handing Connolly her phone. The screen showed Gary Williams' Instagram page.

"Oh my fucking God!" He said when he saw the pic of Gary with Marcus Tanner.

"It looks like Marrow found herself a lead. "Baisley said with pride.

"Yeah now where the hell is Marrow? And who the hell is that other guy?" Connolly wanted to know.

"We have to find that ambulance ASAP." Baisley replied looking at the video again.

"I do not believe it!" Basley said and nearly fainted. "That is Marcus Tanner!" she said still in shock.

Connolly looked at the paused video frame which caught Tanner looking directly at the camera.

In the middle of the night Marcus was up getting updates from Chet via text. Chet assured him that things were not great, but they could have turned out a lot worse. Marrow was sleeping soundly, and Marcus thought of doing the same., when a message came through his phone. Only two people knew his number, and this was not Chet. The message said,

"I want to congratulate you on a job well done. That was a spectacle that will not soon be forgotten. But what is your next move? I myself, am a chess master and I have studied this game from any and every angle, and the outcome is the same. CHECKMATE"

Marcus read the message over and thought about it, and he was right. He was running out of moves. How long could he expect to stay alive and out of prison if he did not find a way out of the country. And as if the sender heard his thoughts a second message appeared. Marcus read it.

"You have no idea how important you have become to people around the world. But I can show you."

When Marcus read the rest of the message, he could not help but smile.

Morning came and Marrow woke up and the sun was already up. She looked up and saw no sign of Marcus.

"Now is my chance!"she said to herself and got up.

Her head was pounding, and the room was spinning but she was determined to escape. She walked through the house and still had no signs of Tanner. When she reached the front door, she saw that the door was cracked open. Marrow peeked out the door half expecting Tanner to pop out of nowhere. But when she went outside in the cool morning air all she could hear was the birds chirping.

She stepped on the sidewalk then she heard engines racing toward her.

Unmarked cars came from all directions.

The SWAT team was right behind them.

"Marrow!"Connolly said as he jumped from one of the unmarked cars.

He reached Marrow and she clasped in his arms.

"I have never been happier to see that face." Marrow said groggily, suddenly dizzy.

Connolly raced her to a car. "Is he still inside?" He asked, kneeling down looking in her eye.

"I don't think so." She responded unsure.

"How did you find me?"

Connolly hesitated then said, "Someone called it in, giving this address saying that you were here." He paused then said, "I think it was him. I think it was Tanner."


*ONE MONTH LATER*
*NEW YORK CITY*

*"Today is the start of the trial of the defendants who have become known as the POPE 5.The main defendant Shawn Butler and his co-defendants have a large list of charges, including plotting to overthrow the government and murder. Security is at an extremely high level due to the fact Mr. Butler is next in command of the POPE movement. He is second only to Marcus Tanner who remains at large. Tanner has not been seen since the march in Washington. In a twist of events a video has been uncovered by MSNBC showing what looks like an execution of a man named Gary Williams at the hands of Washington PD. But in the immediate aftermath of William's death a man who has been identified as Marcus Tanner killed both officers and saved the life of an undercover FBI agent. The agent's identity is being withheld at this time."* The reporter said.

The midtown Manhattan courthouse was a media circus. Federal authorities were taking no chances with the defendants in what was being called the trial of the century. Shawn was inside of a holding cell in the bottom of the courthouse. Surrounded by a small army of U.S. Marshals. Being that Shawn was a lawyer himself he studied his case night and day. And he was smart enough to know that the case against him was far from airtight but that did not mean they would let him win. With all of the publicity that the case had received it would be next to impossible to find someone who was not influenced by all of the coverage.

When Shawn was led into the packed courtroom the place erupted! The crowd was split down the middle. He had his supporters but he also had those who came to see him die for his crimes. Shawn was led in wearing a three piece suit. Though he had lost some weight while he was in custody, he was in the best shape of his life.

Due to the fact that all he did was work on his case and exercise. Seated at the defense table along with him were the other co-defendants in the case.

This was the first time that he had ever laid eyes on any of them. From reading the case he knew them by name.

Evan Oliver, who was in charge of the Philadelphia branch was seated next to him. Next to Oliver was Ernesto 'Nesto' Garcia, who was the head man of the Los Angeles branch. Also at the defense table was Robert Watts and his sister Roberta who together oversaw the Baltimore chapter.

"All rise to the Honorable Valerie Preston presiding." The bailiff said as the judge strode into the courtroom.

"You may be seated." Judge Preston said and sat down.

"Before I bring the jury in I want to lay down some ground rules." Judge Preston began. "I will not tolerate outbursts in my courtroom. Is that clear?" She said looking into the gallery.

"Also I understand the extreme importance of this case and the historical ramifications that it entails. With that said I will keep a short leash on both parties. I will call everything to the absolute letter of the law. Is that clear, counselors?"

"Yes Your Honor" They said almost in unison.

After that the jury was escorted inside the courtroom. Judge Preston said.

"Garrison you may begin your opening statement."

"Thank you Your Honor." Thomas Garrison replied.

Garrison was the Deputy Attorney General, second in command at the Department of Justice.

"Ladies and gentlemen of the jury. You have been summoned here today to help make a statement to the world, that taking the law into your own hands will not be tolerated. That tearing at the fabric that makes this country great, will not be taken lightly. The defendants have decided to declare war on your way of life. They chose to pledge their allegiance to a cold blooded murderer, and help him carry out his murderous agenda. In coordinated attacks across the country, the men and women seated here decided to engage in warfare with the brave men and women who protect this great nation. They have succeeded with dividing the country. But today is your chance to take the first steps in putting it back the way it was! And we can do that by sentencing each and every one of them to the death penalty! True the man who started this misguided crusade is still at large. But these are his most trusted allies and they were complicit in threatening to overthrow the United States government! Therefore there can only be one verdict. GUILTY, GUILTY, GUILTY!" Garrison yelled inciting the police sympathizers.

"Alright! Enough!" Judge intervened, quieting the slight uproar. "The defense may now have their opening argument."

As soon as the words were out of the judge's mouth Andrew Fitzsimmons was like a bull out of the gate.

"I will not bore you with a sermon about justice and how great this country is. Or how upstanding and brave the men and women who protect this country are. The truth of the matter is that justice is not for everyone. That police officers do not protect everyone. That in fact sometimes they even kill the citizens they are sworn to protect. That is what this whole case is about! My opponent said that you should find them guilty and send them to death row. I say that you set them free and throw them a parade! They fought against oppression by any means. Throughout history when people fought tyranny they were hailed as Heroes! From the Boston Tea Party to Patrick Henry declaring, 'Give Me Liberty or give me Death!' What just because they are black and poor, means that they are not entitled to the same rights as those that have come before them? They are what make this country, what it is! People like them are the reason there is a country at all! Sgt. Evan Oliver served two tours of duty and was awarded the Medal of Honor and a Purple Heart. This great country of ours is flawed. And one of the most glaring flaws is that poor and oppressed people die in record numbers. And up until now no one would do anything about it. Until Marcus Tanner came along and said, no more! Marcus Tanner could not be here today because the biggest manhunt in U.S history could not bring him in. Oh and who by the way saved one of the agents assigned to catch him from being murdered by the Washington D.C police. My client was contacted by Mr. Tanner and agreed to help him spread the word. There is no crime in that. And the other defendants were under attack based on the political and social beliefs, and they fought back! That does not make them criminals that make them heroes!"Fitzsimmons pauses to let this sink in.

~~~~

"Please don't kill me!" She pleaded as she looked at the lifeless body of the man next to her.

"Do it!" She heard the other man urge her to be the killer.

243

The feel of the cold steel against the back of her head sent chills down her spine. She knew that in a few short seconds that she would be dead. Then he came. Moving faster than any man should be able to move. She looked helplessly into his eyes. They were the eyes that she had never been able to forget

Marrow awoke from her dream. The same dream that she had been having night after night. Against her protest she was on Administrative leave. They had even forced her to speak with a shrink! As much as she hated to admit it, she knew she needed time off. Be that as it may she could still not shut her mind off. All day all she thought about was how to catch Tanner. And at night all she could think of was how he had saved her life. Thinking about the conversation they had. How when he spoke, how passionate he was. The fire in his eyes burned their way into her memory.

The ringing of her phone snapped her back to reality. It was Connolly.

"Hey there partner."

"What do you want Connolly?" Marrow growled looking at her partner on Facetime.

"Nothing just wanted to see if my better half wanted to go to lunch with me today. On me, what do you say?"

"That is not going to happen because ever since someone leaked that video, the media have been stalking me. They have my apartment staked out non-stop!"

"Marrow I understand that but you have to get out. You have been cooped up in there for weeks and we are starting to worry about you."

Marrow ignored the "We" because she did not want to think about who Connolly might be talking about her to.

"Don't worry I am doing great." She said half lying hoping he brought it.

"I don't buy that for a second. Now I want you showered and dressed. I will be there to get you in exactly one hour." And with that he hung up before she had a chance to protest.

"Damn it!"She said and threw her phone on the bed.

Even though she would never admit it to Connolly, she knew she needed to get out of the house. So she got in the shower and began getting ready. Exactly one hour later Connolly was at her door ringing the buzzer. Marrow buzzed him into the building and he came up stairs. When Marrow opened the door Connolly said,

"Wow!"His eyes opened wide.

"I look that bad? I'm changing."Marrow said and began to walk back in her apartment.

"No, no, you look great!" Marrow was wearing a sundress and some sandals and she had her hair down. "I have never seen you in a dress before."

"Well quit hawking before I change my mind. Besides I figure that if I am going to be on the 6 o'clock news, I might as well be cute."

They went to a bistro in Alexandria where they ordered and talked.

"Seriously, Marrow how are you holding up?" Connolly asked once their food was served. "Actually, I am alright. I am a lot tougher than I look." She replied half joking "What have I been missing at the office since I was out."She asked, changing the subject.

"Well for one, the entire intelligence community is trying to figure out the whereabouts of one Marcus Tanner. It's like he just fell off the map after leaving you in that house." Connolly said looking at Marrow for a reply.

"I think that somehow he made it out of the country. That is the only way that I could see him avoiding detection."

"I think you're onto something with that, and so does the CIA because they have been suggesting that he is overseas some place."

Marrow thought for a second before responding.

"And how are they coming to that conclusion? Let me guess they know about some overseas contact Tanner has." Marrow said, shaking her head.

"His name is Abdul Ibn Aziz. 15th in line for the throne of Saudi Arabia."

"Bastards!" Marrow spat. "Why in the hell wouldn't they share that with us? Now that he is in the wind they tell us! This pissing match between us and them has got to stop before more innocent people die. So now what are we supposed to do?" Marrow said fighting her rising anger.

"We are not going to do anything, but get ready to testify at Butler's trial."

Marrow rolled her eyes.

"You and I both know that he is being held on trumped up charges to prevent the next person from helping Tanner. But guess what? It is too late! He already has over a million people following him! And I ain't talking about Twitter! We know that first hand by how many people showed up on the President's front lawn."

Connolly had never seen her like this before.

"So, what do you think we should do?" He wanted to know.

"I don't know about you, but I do not intend to stop looking for him! I don't care how far he has run, I am not stopping!"

# CHAPTER 10

## SALALAH, OMAN

*T*he sound of the Adhan calling Muslims to their morning prayer stirred Marcus from his sleep. Hearing the call five times a day was somehow soothing to Marcus. Since his arrival he had been bound to the home he was currently a guest in. Not to say that the palatial home was not one of the loveliest he had ever seen. But he was going crazy after being cooped up for over a month.

The night of the March in Washington, Marcus received a text from Abdul Aziz. He proposed a plan and offered Marcus the services of the Saudi embassy. With their assistance he was whisked away on a private jet to Saudi Arabia. But he did not stay there, he changed planes and was off to Oman, where he has remained ever since.

Marcus had no contact with Aziz since he landed, but he had been given word that he would see him shortly.

When Marcus exited his bedroom he was greeted by Yusuf, who was the only person that he had actual contact with.

"As Salaamu Alaykum brother, I pray Allah has blessed you with a good night's sleep."

"I slept very well thank you. But that is pretty much all I have done since I have been here."

Yusuf smiled and replied, "It is Your Highness's wish that your every need be supplied to you, and that you be well rested. The bullet wound that you received is healed nicely."

Marcus moved his shoulder as if he was testing it for pain and replied.

"It feels like new, but my mind is going crazy!"

"I have a message from His Royal Highness. He said that he is under a great deal of scrutiny from your country. He said that it would be unwise for him to meet with you now."

Marcus could see the wisdom in these words. Yusuf, who could see he was still disappointed, said, "Do not despair, after your breakfast Your Highness has arranged a surprise for you."

After eating, Marcus climbed into the back of the Maybach that bore Oman's official seal. A small caravan led the way through the streets of the city. Marcus was intrigued by the vibrant city that was teeming with life. It occurred to him that life here was a lot like life back in America. Marcus wondered if he would ever see it again. Despite its many flaws, it was still the best country on Earth. It just had to treat its poorest and people of color fairly. He was having these thoughts when the car came to a stop. They were at a small airport.

"Your flight awaits you."

A Gulf Stream V was sitting on the runway ready for takeoff. Yusuf escorted Marcus onboard and soon they began taxiing down the runway. After the plane took off and they were at cruising altitude, Yusuf said, "There is something I wish for you to see Mr. Tanner. Some things my words cannot do justice. You have no idea how strong your message is or how it resonated with so many."

Marcus wanted to ask questions but something told him to keep quiet, so he did.

The three-hour flight was passed with Marcus reading about current events. Most of the stories on the front pages were about him. What concerned him the most was, Shawn's trial was underway in New York. His heart went out to Shawn, and he wished it was something that he could do for him. Also he saw a story about the FBI agent he saved. As it turned out she was in charge of the task force that was set up to capture him. Her name was Angelica Marrow. Marcus looked at a picture that had been taken in better days. She was a total knockout. The plane made its descent and soon they were touching down.

"Welcome to the Democratic Republic of the Congo."

Yusuf said as he led the way out of the plane. They were greeted by a caravan of cars and trucks. As they drove Yusuf spoke.

"Nowhere in Africa is saturated in more blood than the Congo. From the late 1800's when the Belgians ruled to today with political and ethnic violence. These are some of the most hopeless people in the world. But all of sudden they have hope.

They have found someone to rally behind. Someone who looks like them. Someone who has made them look at one and another like the brothers they are!"

They were in Kinshasa, the capital of the Congo. The car stopped by a hotel and they got out.

"The man that they have rallied behind is right there."Yusuf said, pointing.

Marcus could not believe what he was looking at. On a wall of a building the opposite of the hotel was a twenty foot tall painting of Marcus! It was from the march. It was the picture that was on the Jumbo -Tron with everyone marching behind him.

"I don't understand how this is possible "Marcus said in awe.

There were people gathered around the painting and when they noticed him, they could not believe it was really him. Dozens of people gathered around him and touched him just to see if he was real. The people started clapping and cheering. They led Marcus through the streets where more people joined them as they made their way through the city. Marcus was led to another painting. This painting was of Martin Luther King, Nelson Mandela and himself.

It was then that he understood the full gravity of who and what he was to these people. Hope.

*NEW-YORK CITY*
*FEDERAL COURTHOUSE*

"Mr. Garrison you may call your next witness to the stand." Judge Preston said.

"Thank you, your Honor. I would like to call Randy Cordell to the stand."

A young black male approached the witness stand and was sworn in.

"Mr. Cordell, what exactly do you do for a living?"

"I am a member of the Los Angeles PD."

"And how long have you served in that capacity?"

"I have been on the force for three years."

"I will get to the heart of the matter. On June 19th of last year, you were involved in an incident, what happened?"

"I was inside the station house doing an arrest report, when out of nowhere an army of heavily armed men stormed the station. They had some of my fellow officers, including the captain as a hostage. They ordered us to put down our weapons."

"Could you tell us what happened next?"

"We were all rounded up and placed inside a holding cell. While we were locked up they hung a gigantic POPE banner from the roof."

"Did they say anything while they held you and your co-workers hostage?"Cordell was quiet for a second and then replied.

"One of them said that they had a message from Marcus Tanner."The courtroom was at attention as they listened to the testimony.

"And what exactly was Mr. Tanner's message?"

"He said that if it was war that we wanted then he would take us to war,"

"No further questions Your Honor."

After a short recess Garrison called Connolly to the stand. He asked Connolly some questions about his background before getting down to business.

"You were one of the lead investigators into the POPE matter?"

"Yes, I was sir. Me and my partner."Connolly quickly replied.

"And where did the investigation lead you as far as the defendants are concerned?"

"They are the hierarchy of Mr. Tanners organization."

"Would you mind elaborating please?" Garrison asked.

"Well...um Mr. Butler was the number two, second only to Tanner himself. It is our view that if not for Butler there would be no organization to speak of. It was he who started organizing and rallying the followers. We believe that Tanner saw this and reached out to Butler and the two of them built the network that is in place today. Along with writing it's doctrine and code of conduct. The other defendants are the heads of just a few of the chapters that are across the country."Garrison walked across the court room and stood by the jury box before saying.

"Based on your opinion how much of a threat are these men and women to society?"

"Objection!" Fitzsimmons said, leaping up.

"Sustained." The judge said before Garrison responded.

"No further questions."

"Your witness." Judge Preston said to Fitzsimmons.

"Agent Connolly I only have a few questions for you."Fitzsimmons said, getting his paperwork in order.

"Do you believe in the Constitution?"

"What? Yes, I believe in the Constitution!"Connolly replied like that was the dumbest thing he had ever heard.

"Well if that is true, then why do you not support my client constitutional right?"

"Objection! Where is all of this going?"

Fitzsimmons said, "I am getting to the very core of this case your Honor."

"Overruled, you may answer."

"And what right is that?"Connolly asked

"The first ,second and fourth to begin with. But we will get to that later. What would you say Mr. Butler's role in all of this was?"

"As I stated earlier he is in a leadership role."Connolly replied calmly.

"And what are his duties in that role?"Connolly was weary and felt a trap coming.

"He helped things along with Marcus Tanner."

"Would you say that he gave orders?"

"Yes."Connolly said simply.

Fitzsimmons nodded his head as if in agreement.

"Do you think he gave the defendants the order to attack the police and the National Guard?"

"Yes, I do. Along with Marcus Tanner." Connolly started to get flustered.

"How would that have been possible if he was in Guantanamo Bay for Christ sakes?" Connolly's face turned beet red.

"Well maybe... um. Maybe he did not give that order. But he was still in charge of the group that carried it out so under the law that makes him guilty."

"Ok let's go with that. He did not give the order but he is in charge of the group. Are you familiar with the second amendment?"

"Of course! It is the right to bear arms."

Fitzsimmons nodded like he agreed but said,

"Exactly but it is much more. It is also the right to a well-regulated Militia being necessary to the security of a free state."

Fitzsimmons paused and let that set into the mind of the jury before proceeding.

"Agent Connolly, you already conceded that my client could not have given the order. And the Constitution gives him the right to regulate, meaning lead a group of armed citizens. So what exactly is my client guilty of?"

"Um….I…um." Connolly stuttered

"Exactly what I thought. No further questions Your Honor."

In the days and weeks following Marcus's trip to Africa, Yusef had shown him that not only the Congo had responded!

"I never thought in my wildest dreams that any of this could have been possible." Marcus said one night while eating dinner with Yusuf in Uganda.

"I will admit I have never seen anything like this as well Mr. Tanner."

"Of all the places you have taken me, nothing had a deeper effect than going to Somalia."

"Excuse me sir, but you had a Dictator pledge himself to you and your cause today!" Yusuf said, taken aback.

The leader of Uganda, Solomon Mtume pledged himself and his country to helping Marcus.

"Don't get me wrong. What happened here today was amazing! But being in Somalia after hearing so many negative stories like pirates and what have you, to feeling nothing but love and acceptance. They carried me on their shoulders and paraded me down the street!" Marcus said, chuckling.

Yusuf smiled at this and said, "It was an amazing sight."

After completing their meal, they went outside to walk it off. The two men continued to talk with their security not too far away. Out of nowhere a van screeched to a stop right beside them. Armed men spilled out.

"What is the meaning of this?" Yusuf demanded but the gunmen seized Marcus and threw a sack over his head and pushed him inside the van and drove away, without a shot being fired. Marcus was trying to keep his cool and figure out what was going on.

"Where are you taking me? Who sent you?"

Were some of the things that Marcus asked that fell on deaf ears. They drove on for hours over rough terrain as well as highways. As tense as the situation was Marcus felt a calm inner peace. If this was the way he was meant to die at least he saw firsthand that his life had made a difference. The van came to a stop. Marcus was led to a waiting truck and loaded inside. They drove for about an hour making one stop. When they stopped again Marcus was roughly grabbed from the back of the truck. The sack was snatched from his head and he was temporarily blinded by the son. He was surrounded by heavily armed men, the man who must have been their leader spoke.

"The Great Marcus Tanner!" he said in heavily accented English. "The man who woke up the sleeping giant and caused the white man many sleepless nights!" He said chuckling but his eyes were not smiling. "From the stories, I expected you to be seven feet tall and carved from stone!" He replied and he and all of his men began laughing. "But you're just another black American man. A nigger as you Americans like to say." the man hissed.

"I assure you this is no ordinary man standing before you." Replied another man dressed in a simple beige tunic.

"Please excuse my associate, Mr. Adinu Jafari. The leader of Boko Haram. And in case you haven't guessed by now I am-" Marcus cut him off and said.

"You are Ibn Abdul Aziz. The man I owe a deep debt of gratitude."Aziz dismissed the last statement with a wave of his hand.

"It is I who owes you Mr. Tanner. You have breathed life in the fight against oppression! You have lit the fire that is burning all over the world now. I have funded the movement for freedom, true freedom since I was old enough to understand what was taking place. It's mostly been what the West likes to call 'Radical Islam'."

"You mean terrorism."Marcus stated flatly.

"That is another Western term. Is it not terrorism when their Reaper drones drop Hellfire missiles that land in crowded urban areas? Is it not terrorism to ignite unrest in a region and instigate sectarian violence? Is it not terrorism to rip people from the only home they ever known and kill those that object?" Marcus could not disagree with anything that he said.

"There is truth to what you are saying, but I disagree with some of the methods used."

"Ah the methods."Ibn Aziz replied. "The methods are exactly why you are here. The methods you have employed have made the world take notice!"Aziz said looking Marcus in the eye. "Tell me something Marcus. What would you do if you had a worldwide organization ready to follow your every command?"

Marcus thought and then said, "I would give the oppressors the fight of their lives." He replied seriously.

"That is exactly what I thought you would say." Aziz said with a smile.

### SEVERAL WEEKS LATER

"This just in. We have just received several video messages from well known terror organizations. Here is Adinu Jafari." The video showed the terror leader standing in front of the black and white POPE flag.

"I hereby renounce all violent action against all innocent civilians. I also pledge my support to the *POOR OPPRESSED PEOPLE EVERYWHERE* movement and it's leader Marcus Tanner."

Marrow watched the news report as she drank her morning coffee, getting ready for what was supposed to be her first day back at work. She grabbed her keys and phone and rushed out the door.

When Marrow arrived at FBI headquarters

"Welcome Back." several of her co-workers said to her.

When she made it to her desk, Connolly was there waiting.

"Happy to have you back." He said to her but Marrow waved him off.

"Fuck the welcome, tell me how Tanner got all of the big wigs in the Middle East to unite and pledge to him? He has nine of the FBI's ten most wanted all signed up!" Marrow was dumbfounded. "Can you tell me how this is possible? I mean it's like Freddy Kruger, Jason Voorhees, Michael Myers and Satan all on the same team for fucks sake!" Marrow said getting angry at the thought.

"It's great having you back." Connolly said, smiling.

Marrow rolled her eyes and said nothing.

"You have got to see this!" Yelled an agent named Thompson. On the television was a video of Marcus Tanner.

"Today is a great day in the fight against oppression. All around the world we have joined forces to fight our common enemy. While we have different approaches and ideology, we have one goal and that is to end all forms of oppression."

With this latest revelation the authorities were in an uproar. The President was not at all happy and he let his displeasure be known.

"This is where I draw the line god damn it!" The President barked in his morning intelligence briefing. "This son of a bitch has somehow managed to form a united nation of terrorism! How in the hell did we allow this to happen, Ned?"

The National Security advisor responded,

"Um, sir the honest truth is that we really don't know. But the overall consensus is that Abdul Ibn Aziz, who we have long thought to be a sponsor of terrorism, has used his influence to bring the various groups together."

The President looked perplexed

"How the hell is that even possible? These bastards are Islamic extremists with the goal of making the world one big Islamic state. What do they have in common with Tanner and his band of idiots?"

Mitch Davies, head of the CIA answered. "Mr. President, Tanner is the focal point of almost nonstop media coverage. He is trending all over social media. Because of what happened right here in D.C, he is a rock star! We all know that he is just the latest nut job to come out of the woodwork, but to them? To people in that part of the world….he is some kind of Messiah. And that makes him more dangerous than any other man who has ever walked the face of the earth."

The President paled after that latest statement.

"What are our options?" the President wanted to know.

"We must neutralize him at any cost. Because I am sorry to say but we have underestimated him. He is the embodiment of our greatest fears. A man who can rally the masses around the world! Poor, middle class. White, black, and brown. Christians, Muslims and Atheists alike. He is gaining power and pretty soon he will become impossible to stop. Because even if we kill him his message will reverberate throughout history."

The President is ashamed. "Jesus Christ!"

Mitch Davies looked him in the eye and said, "Exactly."

Marrow was arriving home after a very, very long day. She was just putting her key in the front door of her building when a black Suburban pulled up. A man got out of the passenger side and walked up to her.

"Agent Marrow, I need you to go inside and pack a bag as quickly as you can."

She calmly replied. "I am sorry but who are you?"

"I am the man who is going to lead you to Marcus Tanner." Marrow thought for a second, and did not say another word.

She went inside and packed her bag.

Marrow, Baisley and Connolly were being briefed in the cabin of Air Force 2.

"How nice of the Vice President to loan us his plane." Connolly said getting comfortable.

"This is the President's way of showing us that this mission is of the highest priority." Said Clint Ward, the man who had brought all of them here in the cover of night,

"Our latest Intel has Tanner traveling all over Africa and the Middle East. Almost every dictator, rebel leader or known terrorist, who has ever had any beef with America and her allies are all *hopping* on Tanner's bandwagon.

Marrow mulled over what Ward had just laid out.

"Alright I get what their play is. They are getting with a winning team. But this cannot be going over well with the hardcore Islamic fanatics. A kufar? An American Kufar at that." Marrow said, referring to the Islamic term for a non-believer.

"And that is exactly what we are hoping for. If we can just find a couple of unhappy campers, maybe just maybe they can lead us to Tanner."Ward said before adding, "It's gonna be a long flight, so if I were you I would get as much sleep as I could. There is no telling when you may be able to sleep again depending on the situation on the ground."

Marrow decided to take his advice and she got as comfortable as she could. Marrow had just closed her eyes when a thought came to her mind. This is it. This is where all of this ends. She didn't know if it was because she'd catch Tanner, kill him or if he killed her.

## NEW-YORK CITY
## FEDERAL COURTHOUSE

Today was closing arguments in the trial of the POPE 5. The government's case was solid but the defense had been top notch. Garrison had already given his closing arguments and now it was Fitzsimmons' turn to give his summation.

"Ladies and gentlemen of the jury, you have sat here day after day, week, after week and now it is time to render a verdict. This trial is one of the most important in the history of the world! No pressure."Fitzsimmons said and got a few laughs. "But seriously, the fact that people are still being killed because of the color of their skin is unacceptable! That is what this trial boils down to. A man stood up and took a stand against the unjust murders of unarmed civilians most notably black men! The defendants heard the call to action and they stood alongside Mr. Tanner and helped in the fight against oppression. Maybe you don't agree with the tactics or the methods that were used, but if not that then what? While we are sitting doing nothing, they did something! This is not a black issue or a white issue. This is a human issue. In the 21st century people should not have to worry about being shot or choked to death by the police based on the color of their skin. There have been far too many legal lynching's. The system has failed those poor people. I will say this in closing, every since Marcus Tanner aka the POPE started his crusade against the injustice in this country, there has not been one murder of unarmed civilians. Maybe you don't agree with the methods but you can't argue with the results. Nothing further your Honor."


## MOGADISHU, SOMALIA

Marcus was eating and enjoying the company of his host.

"Mr. Tanner, I welcome you to my home and my country. "Replied Festus Okwasi, the richest man in Somalia.

Okwasi was a telecommunication mogul.

"You have a lovely home and a lovely country." Marcus replied.

"Mr. Tanner, the people of my country love you. You have given them something that they have never known and that is hope. They will fight for you and they will lay down their lives for you if need be."

"And that is the reason that I have decided to make Somalia my base of operation."

"I think that would be a very wise decision on your part Mr. Tanner." Replied Okwasi. "Mogadishu is a virtual fortress! The only way that they would dare enter is with the entire U.S military." Marcus knew that there was some truth to what he was saying.

"With the proper training I think that they can hold their own with any army in the world." Marcus said, distracted by the entrance of Ibn Aziz and Aminu Jafari.

"Marcus, As Salam Alaikum."Aziz said to which Marcus replied,

"Walaikum Salaam."

Jafari just gave a curt nod.

"I take it that you are talking about the plan to make this the base of our operation?" Aziz asked.

"We were, as a matter of fact." Marcus replied.

"The arms that you requested have arrived and are waiting to be off loaded."Aziz informed him.

"Why does this one need guns? He is making promises that we will not fight! We are like a dog that has had his balls snipped!" Jafari sneered.

"I made no such promise. I said that we would not target innocent civilians." Marcus said evenly. "I think that you are afraid of the white devil! I think that you are not what people think you are?"

"Jafari! That will be enough." Aziz said, staring daggers into Jafari.

"Jafari, what we are trying to do is to turn third world nations into super powers! Because there will never be true equality without economic equality. We could all die in war against the oppressors but if we build up a nation that can live on for hundreds of years, we win." Marcus said, trying to reach Jafari.

"I know nothing of what you talk about. I only know how to fight." And with that Jafari walked away.

"People are afraid of the unknown." Aziz explained simply as he watched Jafari walk away. "Fear can either push you forward or it holds you back. Let's pray he pushes forward."Marcus said.

266

He was starting to think Jafari may become a problem.

## ADEN, YEMEN

When Marrow and her team arrived in Yemen they were greeted by a representative from the State Department.

"I'm Hank Portis and I will be your point man on this case."

Besides Marrow, Baisley, Connolly, Ward and some of his associates from the CIA who mostly kept to themselves. The Yemen government also had the Yemen defense forces on hand, just in case things got hairy.

"There is definitely a buzz in the air." Potis began. "We are not sure what it is but the whole region is starting to brace itself for whatever is about to happen."

"Alright where do we start?" Connolly asked.

"I have an asset in the area who can probably point us in the right direction." Ward replied vaguely.

They arrived in a residential neighborhood. People eyed them with suspicion as they drove past the curious residents. The house that they stopped at was identical to all the rest of the houses in the area.

" I need one of you to come with me, I don't care which." Ward said getting out of the truck. Connolly and Baisley nodded at Marrow acknowledging that she should go. Marrow got out and followed Ward, who was at the front door of the house. Ward knocked and it was answered by a teenage boy.

"Ahmed, can we talk?" Ward said and shouldered his way in the door. The home was neat and tidy. Ahmed seemed to be the only one home at the time.

"This is Agent Marrow from the FBI and she has some questions she wants to ask you." Ward says and motions toward Marrow.

"What is going on Ward?" Marrow asked, referring toward the strange way that he was acting.

"Ahmed is the end all, be all, in matters related to Marcus Tanner in these parts." Marrow was starting to get it.

"Where is Marcus Tanner?" she asked.

"I could not tell you." Amhed said simply without any traces of an accent. Marrow believed him and moved on.

"What is he up to? What is going on that has everyone in frenzy." She asked.

Ahmed smiled and said. "He is attempting to make right, what has been wrong for a millennia." He answered cryptically.

"What the hell is that supposed to mean?"

" It means that he is assembling that which scares you the most." After several more attempts to get him to answer a straight question Marrow gave up. When they were outside Marrow asked.

"What gives? We're wasting time talking to that fucking retard! He gave us a squat! Let's say we get serious and really put some effort into catching Tanner!"

"Trust me Marrow I would not waste your time. Ahmed is a little different but he has always proved helpful. You see he was shot in the head by a stray bullet when he was a young child. He healed completely but he had…..visions." Ward said cryptically.

"Visions? Are you fucking kidding me?"

"No." Ward said seriously. Ward did not strike her as the type that would subscribe to such things. "That kid saved my life before with something that he told me. If I had any doubts before that they were removed when that suicide bomber walked into my office and blew himself to bits."

Marrow did not know what to say.

"Whatever he said you can take it to the bank! We just have to find out what the hell it meant!"


### AL JAWF, LIBYA

"Marcus it is an honor to meet you." Replied the much older man.

"I have heard a great deal about you." Marcus said in reply.

"You cannot believe everything that you hear, young warrior." The older man replied.

"I have heard that you are the wisest man in all of Africa."Marcus said honestly.

"Wisdom comes from living long enough to make mistakes and learn from them. And God knows I have lived long and I have made a great deal of mistakes." The man said laughing.

"Ali Bin Wafasi, I have come to seek your counsel." Marcus said seriously.

" I am aware of that. What is it that you ask of me?" Marcus thought for only a second and then said with conviction.

"I believe that it is my mission to fight oppression around the world. But how can I fight this fight and win?"

Ali Bin Wafasi was thoughtful before answering.

"In order to solve any problem. Or to stop any behavior you must get to the root of that problem. The root of oppression is right here."

He said pointing to the ground.

"This land has been oppressed because that was God's will. He made this land so rich and plentiful, that greedy men from around the world came in search of her many treasures. When the outsiders came, they were welcomed with open arms but it did not take long for their true nature to come to the surface. The only way for our people to be free. And I mean the truest form of freedom, you must liberate Africa first! Everything that you need to successfully conquer oppression and the oppressor is right here in

Africa! And how do we know this? Because everything that they got from here, they used to build themselves an empire!"

When Marcus was done talking to Ali Bin Wafasi he felt light headed like he was drunk. The thoughts that were moving through his mind quickly came together in a plan that was so audacious, yet so simple. Marcus climbed into the back of the Land Rover where Ibn Aziz awaited him.

"Was it everything that I said it would be?" Aziz asked.

Marcus was still somewhat in a daze.

"I have a plan. I want you to listen to everything that I have to say before you speak."

Ibn Aziz nodded.

"We must liberate Africa. He said that this was the root of the oppression of our people. There is a reason why my message has reached the people of the Motherland. It is because they have been waiting. Waiting for me and for us to come and set them free! We have every country on the continent already supporting our entire movement. Now it is time to step it up. And here is how we are going to do it!"


### SANAA,YEMEN

In the weeks that Marrow had been in Yemen, were some of the most frustrating of her life. In that time there had been at least twenty credible sightings of Marcus Tanner. It was almost like he was not hiding but was out and about loving his newfound celebrity status.

"Hey partner I got something from over the wire that is supposed to be somehow connected to Tanner, but I don't see it." Connolly said, handing her the report.

"This is about jets being brought from the Russians. What the hell could that have to do with having to do with Tanner?" Marrow asked.

She continued to read and saw why it had been flagged.

"The purchase was flagged because it was by a front company with ties tolbn Aziz!" Marrow jumped to her feet."I want anything that even remotely connects to this."Marrow said pointing to the papers.

Several hours later they were swamped with paperwork.

"What the hell are they up too?" Baisley asked as she read the reports.

They showed that several shell companies had made purchases. Ward came to the office door and said,

"I think I know what's going on but you are not going to believe it. It looks like Tanner is going to every African country and .....trying to unite them. I mean like really unite them! As in one huge country!" He said and the implications were clear to Marrow right away.

"A huge country with a huge army!" Marrow said.

But then she thought about what Ahmed had said to her.

"This is what he was talking about!" Marrow said looking at Ward. "He is fixing what has been wrong for a millennia and he is assembling what we fear the most! Not only a huge army, but a huge black army!"

## WASHINGTON D.C

The President was clearly not doing well.

"What do you have for me?" He asked almost afraid of what he was going to hear.

"Our latest Intel has shown that Tanner is in Africa and he is trying to gather support." Said his National Security advisor.

 "Support for what?" The President asked wearily.

"Ah.. support for one African state. He is trying to unite all of the African Nations under one banner."

The President's face was ashen.

"I do not care what you have to do, I want that son of a bitch dead!"

"I call this meeting of the African Union to order." Said the Chairperson. "The committee recognizes the President of Nigeria Fellipe Naji."

"Thank you Chairperson. I have called this emergency meeting, because there is something that needs to be brought to the table and voted on today. The unrest that has started in America and made its way around the world is the reason that I call you here today. We had noble reasons for starting the African Union, but I am here to say that it has been a failure. We have failed the people who look to us for leadership. We have failed our ancestors who have lived, died and bled so that we may be here today. The world is changing! And we must lead the way into the future! This is the richest continent on the planet, yet our people live in poverty! We fight among one another over trivial differences. Those days are over. Because today we will become brothers in every sense of the word. I have had the pleasure of meeting the man that has been responsible for the change that the world is seeing. I know that some of you have met him as well, but I invited him today. Everyone Marcus Tanner."

The crowd all gasped in surprise. Marcus walked out in a three-piece suit.

"Brothers it is an honor to be here with you today. I will not waste any time because even as I stand here with you our enemy is only a few steps behind. I will start by saying that, for a long time I was blinded by my oppressors. I was taught that I was different from you. I was taught that you would not accept me because I was born in America. But those were all lies! I am you and you are me. I have felt loved and embraced the second I stepped foot in this land, the Motherland! Today we must unite! We must turn Africa into the Superpower she was meant to be! We have made every nation around the world rich while we starved and begged for scraps! But we will stop that today by voting to unite as one! The oppressors lied and made laws that would protect them and keep us in servitude. We will repeal and replace any law that was put into place to keep us down. We will expel the Oppressor from our land. All business that has profited from our blood and sweat will be seized! We will build weapons that will deter any future strikes against us or our people!" This last statement caused a stir.

"You can't be talking about... nuclear weapons!" Replied President Mohamad Kaguta of Namibia.

"That it is precisely what I am talking about." Marcus admitted.

"This is madness!" Mohamad Kaguta shouted. "How are we supposed to get uranium? And who is going to give us the technology to enrich the uranium to weaponize it? Because of the Non Proliferation Act no one is going to give us the technology to build a nuclear weapon." Kaguta stated matter of fact.

"The answer to your first question is literally right under your feet. Africa is the most mineral rich continent and uranium is no exception. It is mostly unexplored but it is there, more than we will

275

ever need. And to answer your second question about where we will get the technology from. I will let the President of South Africa answer that."

And with that President Anwar Bocte took the floor.

"I first off want to say that I do not enter in to this agreement lightly. I know that the world is undergoing a seismic shift. I also know that those who profit from our oppression will stop at nothing to keep us from uniting and becoming a Superpower. But it is for this reason that I offer the technology necessary to secure our future. My country built six nuclear weapons in the late 80's and early 90's.We were in the final stages of completing a $7^{th}$ when we were persuaded to scrape our nuclear program by the United Nation, because they knew that a black President would soon be elected and they did not want that kind of power in the hands of a Blackman."

Bacote was quiet for a few seconds while he let the last statement sink in. "In the years since I have become President, I have learned a great deal about the secrets of my country's past. I have learned that the technology that you need is still available to you. Also we have a working nuclear plant and reactor. And lastly the 7 weapons that were thought destroyed are in fact in a secure location and are fully operational." The meeting erupted.

"We can rewrite history today. It is entirely possible to alter the fate of an entire race of people today depending on how you vote.

Thank you for taking the time to hear me out." Marcus said in conclusion.

Marcus left them to take their vote.

"In a stunning development, the African Union has formalized an agreement to unite all 55 countries of Africa into one. I repeat the African Union voted unanimously to unite all 55 countries of Africa into one country!" The reporter said on the news.

"What the hell just happened?" Marrow said miserably.

"We are always a day late and a dollar short when it comes to this guy."Connolly said with frustration.

"He has been lucky a whole lot. I will admit that, but all we need is to get lucky one time! And then his ass will be grass!" Ward replied.

Just then his phone rang.

"What? When? We will be right there." Ward said and hung up.

"Let's move." Ward said rushing out the door.

Everyone quickly followed.

"Remember what we said about all we needed was one unhappy camper to give us the break we need?"

"Yeah." Marrow replied, waiting in suspense. "

Well I just got a call stating that a high value target has agreed to help us by giving information about the whereabouts of one Marcus Tanner!" Ward said with a rare smile on his face.

"Who is it?" Baisley asked. "Who is this high value target?"

"You will not believe it if I told you. It will be better if you saw him for yourself.

## NEW YORK CITY
## FEDERAL COURTHOUSE

The jury had been deliberating for a week. Shawn's nerves were shot from waiting on the verdict.

"What the hell is taking them so long?" Shawn wanted to know.

"Shawn I will tell you that the longer it takes the better it is for your chances of winning." Fitzsimmons said.

Shawn had to come to court everyday while the jury went through the steps of trying to reach a verdict.

"I have some news for you Shawn." Fitzsimmon said.

Shawn automatically assumed the worst.

"What happened? Is it about Marcus?" Fitzsimmons put his head down and nodded his head.

"What happened?"

"Ah it would seem that Marcus has done the impossible!"Fitzsimmons said with a huge grin. "Marcus left the country and went to Africa and the Middle East. Not only did he convince terror groups to renounce but also to pledge to him and POPE. But that is not the amazing part. Marcus was able to

278

convince the African Union to merge all the countries of Africa into one!"Shawn could not believe what he was hearing.

"I can't, How is that possible?" Shawn asked in awe.

"I don't know how he did it but he has the rest of the world shaking in their boots!"

Fitzsimmons said with a mischievous grin.

"Butler." A Marshal said peeking is head into the cell block.

"Get ready the jury is back with a verdict."

Shawn was more nervous than he had ever been in his life.

"You ready?" Fitzsimmons asked.

"As ready as I am going to get." Shawn said and got ready to go into the courtroom.

Thoughts flooded Shawn's mind in the minutes leading up to the jury announcing the verdict. He had a chance to be a part of history. He knew that nothing they could do to him would be able to change that. Marcus had achieved great things and none of them would have been possible without him he thought. There was the very real possibility that he would live the rest of his life in a cage. But if he had to do it all over again, he would. Judge Preston sat up on the bench looking down at him. Shawn walked in and stood before the judge. As the jury walked in he tried to make eye contact but none of them would look at him. He did not take that as a good sign.

"Ladies and Gentleman of the jury, have you reached a verdict?"

"We have your Honor." Replied the foreman of the jury.

"And what is that verdict."

"We find the defendant," The packed courtroom held their collective breath.

~~~~

When Marrow, Connolly, Bailey and Ward arrived at the location the meeting was set to take place, it was deserted.

"This doesn't feel right. It could be some type of ploy to lure us out into the open." Connolly said aloud.

"I don't like it, I don't like it but -" Marrow was cut short when she heard what she thought was a cell phone ringing. "Where is that coming from? Find that phone."

The four of them looked and Marrow quickly found it and answered. It was a video call.

"I am glad that you could join me." Marrow could not believe who was on the other line. Aminu Jafari.

"I hope you are not pulling my chain." Ward replied to the terrorist leader.

"I assure you that I am not, as you say pulling your chain."

"You say you got intel on Tanner? Well where is he?" Marrow said getting to the point.

"I do indeed know his current location but there are a few details we have to discuss before you get your prize."Jafari said.

"And what is that you want?" Marrow asked.

"What I want is the twenty million dollar reward that you have offered, for starters. Also, I want immunity and asylum in the United States."

"What? No that is never going to happen." Ward barked.

"It is my final offer. Take it or leave it." Jafari stated with confidence.

"Hold on." Marrow said, hitting the mute button."I don't see what other choice we have. The President said do whatever we have to do....well this seems like something we have to do!" Marrow said not liking it one bit.

"We can't give this psychopath asylum in the States! He is a butcher who slaughtered people for little to no reason at all!" Baisley said incuriously.

"We don't have much of a choice do we?" Marrow stated

She hit the mute button.

"I can get you the 20 million. I may even get you immunity but there is no way that I can go to the President and tell him I want to set a killer like you lose in the US. It ain't happening. But I can set you up somewhere else, let me work on it."

Marrow said with her fingers crossed. "I will accept this, but if you try anything, you will never find Tanner. I look forward to hearing from you within the hours with the details." Jafari demanded and disconnected the line.


Marrow was on a conference call with the White House.

"Sir we have an asset that says that he can give us the location of Marcus Tanner within the hour."

"That's excellent news! So what is the hold up? Let's get this scumbag as soon as possible."

"Well sir the asset is Aminu Jafari."

"What? I don't believe it!" The President said, shocked.

"Yes sir, he wants the 20 million reward. Also, he wants immunity and asylum in the United States."

"Absolutely not! I will not have that monster on American soil unless it is in a supermax prison!"

"I told him as much sir. I told him that we can work on asylum in another country. But the other demands sir?"

The President thought for a while then asked the Director of the CIA Mitch Davis.

"What do you think?"

"I think it's the only thing to do." He said simply.

"How sure are we about the intel?"

"We will check everything out as soon as we get the information." Marrow said.

"Alright, but I want this kept top secret! Am I clear? I don't need it getting out that I made a deal with one maniac to get rid of another."

"Thank you sir. I will update you as soon as anything develops."

"Let's go and get this fucker!"

The deal with Jafari was done, now was the moment of truth. The money was wired to a numbered account and Jafari answered the twenty-million-dollar question.

"Where is he Jafari?" Marrow asked.

He smiled an evil smile at her and said,

"He is in Somalia."

"It is almost impossible to move the amount of troops needed to take him down without arousing any suspicion."Ward said.

"Somalia was a great choice for him to set up his operation. He is surrounded by a little over 11 million people who worship him and look at him as their savior. We can't send troops in there."Ward said shaking his head.

"I'm sorry to say but we are out of it. The word came from the White House that we are to stand down and let the military handle it from here."Ward said, bracing himself for what he knew was coming.

"What? What the hell is this shit?" Marrow said walking toward Ward.

"Marrow we won! We did a great job! We are about to get him, isn't that what you wanted?"Ward asked.

It was what she wanted but she wanted the privilege of bringing him in. But she knew he was right. This was bigger than her and what she wanted. It was only a matter of time before Tanner was dead or in a jail cell.

Marcus was working on his plan to help with the transition of power with the new African government. He had been so busy lately that he had not been keeping up with his social media accounts. When he looked he was floored by what he saw.

## "SHAWN BUTLER NOT GUILTY"

Marcus could not believe his eyes!

He quickly called Chet.

"Marcus, Marcus he won Marcus!"Chet said excitedly.

"It's crazy here! I am at the courthouse now!"Chet said


*WASHINGTON D.C*
*THE WHITE HOUSE*

"Sir we have a satellite over the coordinates that Jafari provided." Replied the Joint Chief of Staff.

"Have we confirmed that it's him yet?" The President wanted to know.

"Not yet sir. But whoever it is there are armed guards there to protect him."

"I want a drone in position, so that as soon as we have confirmation, I want him blown to bits!" The President ordered.

*Freedom!*

Shawn couldn't really believe that he was actually free! When the jury came back with a not guilty verdict, he thought that he was hearing things. But when the courtroom exploded and a fight broke out with the cops and the POPE supporters, he knew he had beat them. Shawn walked out of the courtroom a free man. When Shawn made it to the courthouse steps there was a mass of people waiting. The crowd roared when they saw him! Shawn put his right fist in the air and the crowd cheered uncontrollably. Chet was at the front of the crowd and he walked up to Shawn and introduced himself.

"Shawn it is an honor to finally meet you. My name is Chet Graham. I have a message from Marcus." Shawn smiled and thought of his friend.

"Tell me what is he up to?" Shawn asked with a smile.

"He is changing the world, what else."Chet said with all seriousness.

Marcus walked onto his balcony to think. He was happy. Everything was going better than he could have ever hoped for. His plan in Africa was coming together. He had managed to wake up the brothers and sisters in America. And Shawn was free! He felt like they could not be stopped. As he was having these thoughts his phone rang.

## WASHINGTON, D.C
## WHITEHOUSE

"Sir I think we have visual confirmation!" Replied a Presidential aide.

"What the hell do you mean, you think? Is it him or not god damn it!"The President yelled.

The aide got back on the phone as they all watched the screen in the Situation Room that showed where they were told Marcus was hiding.

"Yes, sir it's him!"

"Well what the hell are you waiting for? Fire!"

"Aziz! Brother I am happy to hear from you." Marcus began.

"Marcus you have to listen to me. You have to get out of there now! Jafari has betrayed you!" Marcus did not bother to think he reacted.

He ran back into the house. As he reached the stairs heading down the building was rocked by a massive explosion. He looked up in time to see the ceiling falling. Marcus was knocked to the floor where he was pinned. He could hear the house collapsing all around him. Then there was nothing but darkness.

## WASHINGTON, D.C
## WHITE HOUSE

"Direct hit! We got him Sir!" Replied the White House Chief of staff.

"We don't know that! I don't want one word of this until we pluck through that rubble and pull his body out. And I want DNA evidence and when that is confirmed and only then will we announce that he is dead. I will not make the same mistake twice."

Marcus was home. He was in his yard laying in the grass. He was so tired that it felt good just to lay here and watch his little brother play. Marcus looked and saw his parents on the porch and they looked happy. Mikey seemed to notice him for the first time and walked over to him.

"What are you doing here?" He asked.

"I'm tired Mikey, and I missed you."Marcus replied.

Mikey shook his head but said nothing.

"You don't belong here."Mikey said looking in Marcus' eyes.

"But I am tired. I just want to sleep."Marcus protested.

"NO! Get up Marcus!"


To be Continued!!!